To Della

A HORSE CALLED SEPTEMBER

Anne Digby

A HORSE CALLED
SEPTEMBER

LONDON : DENNIS DOBSON

Copyright © 1976 by Pat Davidson
All rights reserved

First published in Great Britain 1976 by
Dobson Books Ltd, 80 Kensington Church Street, London, W8
Printed in Great Britain by
Bristol Typesetting Co, Ltd,
Barton Manor, St Philips, Bristol

ISBN O 234 77875 X

CONTENTS

ONE

BAD NEWS FOR MARY

Anna broke the bad news to Mary on a Thursday evening. Mary was just inside the stable giving September some oats. Anna's words, spoken slowly, shocked her.

Only then did she realize that she had been foolish to believe that things would never change on Chestnut Farm, that such a happy way of life could go on for ever.

Of course, she should have guessed. Anna's father owned Chestnut Farm and Mary's father worked for him as his cowman. The Dewars lived in the lovely thatched Devon farmhouse and their fields and woods rolled southward over the hill as far as the eye could see and down to the sea beyond. Mary Wilkins and her father lived in a small cottage down the muddy lane past the cow sheds; it went with the job.

The differences had never bothered the two girls. Neither had any brothers or sisters and they had grown up together on the lonely farm, glad of each other's friendship. When they were little, Mr Dewar had bought two ponies so that they could ride to the village school together by way of the bridleway that skirted the wooded hill. It was over four miles by way of the road.

That was how their great love of riding had begun.

When they were eleven they transferred to Silverstock Comprehensive School in a distant market town and were no longer able to ride to school, but instead were picked up from the end of the lane by school bus each morning at ten minutes to eight.

Shortly after they left the village school, Mr Dewar sold the two ponies. Mary had fought to keep 'her' pony, Pickle.

'*Please*, Dad,' she had begged. 'We could buy Pickle from Mr Dewar and keep him in our wood shed, it's plenty big enough.'

'And what would we buy him with?' asked John Wilkins.

'With my post office savings of course, Dad.' Mary had put away birthday money and Christmas money and odd-job money for years. 'I've nearly forty pounds.'

'The pony would cost every penny of that,' said her father. 'In any case, you need that money by you. There'll be all sorts of things you'll be wanting once you've been at your new school a while. You'll want to keep up with the others, I daresay.'

'No, I won't!' Mary had protested. 'There's nothing I could ever want compared with buying Pickle and having him for my own. I'm sure Mr Dewar wouldn't want more than thirty-five pounds for him, seeing he's half mine already. And it's *my* money, Dad—'

'Have you ever thought how much it costs to keep a horse?' asked her father quietly. 'We'd have to feed the animal, apart from all the extras and you never know when you'll need to call the vet in. Mr Dewar's looked after all that up to now, let you have the use of the pony all these years, so that you two girls could get to school. You should count yourself lucky—'

'*Please*, Dad. You're being mean. There must be ways you could save money.'

'Hold your tongue, child!' John Wilkins was a big man and slow to anger, but he was angry now. 'I'm surprised at you, thinking I could afford it for you to have a pony of your own. Where do you get such grand ideas from?

8

You've no need of a pony now, and that's the end of it.'

It was different for Anna. Although she was sad to say goodbye to her pony, she was excited at the same time. Her father had promised to buy her a proper horse, a show-jumper, in its place. Both girls had shown a great talent for show-jumping and carried off many prizes on Pickle and Prune at local gymkhanas. No matter how busy he was at the farm, Mr Dewar always found time to come and watch his daughter perform. He believed that Anna had a great future in front of her as a show-jumper, and the new horse was to be the first step along the road.

'He may not look much, and he's not been schooled too well, but he's got the makings of a magnificent jumper,' said Mr Dewar, the day he bought the horse. 'You'll see. They're bringing him over tomorrow.'

Anna couldn't wait to tell Mary the news. She ran through the farmyard and past the cowsheds, where John Wilkins was busy milking, and down the lane to Primrose Cottage. She burst into the sitting-room, where Mary was getting the fire to light. Her father would soon be back for his supper and now that it was September he liked to eat in front of a warm fire.

'He's coming tomorrow! The new horse—'

She saw the wistful look on Mary's face, and knelt down on the floor beside her, putting an arm round her shoulders.

'*Our* new horse,' she said. 'You know we're going to share him, the way we've always shared everything.'

Mary, who was still missing Pickle badly, felt better after that. She did not even mind that Anna, who was thoughtless about such things, had brought a whole lot of farmyard mud into the sitting room with her, and she just had time to brush it up into the dustpan before her father came in for his supper.

The next day Mary helped Anna clean out the stable in readiness for the new arrival. She lingered over the job

9

as long as possible, anxious not to miss its coming. At last the horse-box drew up in the farmyard and the big animal was brought gently down the ramp. For Mary, it was love at first sight. He was a long-legged rather gawky looking horse, certainly not very beautiful. But there was something quite endearing about him, all the more so because, being a highly-strung animal, his legs had been bound up for the journey with wads of cotton wool beneath the hooves, so that he looked rather like a horse in bedsocks.

He shrank back nervously from Anna's first touch and Mary could tell at once that she was disappointed. She had dreamt about his arrival for so long, studied pictures of many beautiful thoroughbred horses and watched the famous show-jumpers in action on television. Now she felt let-down.

' He—he looks rather ordinary, a bit clumsy,' she said. 'Are you sure he can jump, Daddy?'

'Quite sure,' said Mr Dewar. 'I've had my eye on him for quite a long time. I told you he wasn't much to look at.'

'*I* think he's beautiful,' said Mary.

Mr Dewar, who usually hardly noticed Mary, gave her a brief smile.

'I expect Anna will let you ride him sometimes.'

After her first disappointment, Anna was determined to make a champion of the horse. She gave him a new name —September—because that was the month he came to live with them at Chestnut Farm, and because his coat was dappled russet and brown, like autumn leaves.

From the start, true to her promise, she tried to share him with Mary in every possible way. He had fallen into bad habits, especially the way he held his head when jumping. In fact at first he was a little reluctant to jump at all. The girls quickly realized that his mouth had been badly jagged at some time by a novice jumper and it was

10

mainly due to Mary's patience that he was cured.

She took him over jumps barely a foot high to start with, holding on to a strap she had fastened round his neck so that his head was completely free as he jumped. Before long she was able to dispense with the strap and hold the reins with just the right amount of gentle pressure required as they jumped. Within a few weeks September was holding his head correctly and jumping beautifully for both girls.

That had all been a long time ago. On the Thursday when Anna broke the bad news to Mary, a sunny spring day towards the end of the Easter holidays, there was a magnificent rosette marked "1st" pinned to September's stable door. It had been won the previous day at a local gymkhana in the major show-jumping event of the day.

The days when Anna and Mary had competed in children's events on their ponies seemed far off now. To Mr Dewar's delight Anna was now one of the leading young show-jumpers in the county, competing against adults and regularly winning cups and money prizes.

Mary was given less chance to ride September these days, and rarely to jump him, on Mr Dewar's orders. But the thrill of accompanying Anna to events, helping to groom the horse beforehand and taking pleasure in their successes, was somehow compensation enough.

On the Thursday morning the two girls walked down to the bay to collect mussels, having put September out to graze.

'He deserves a quiet day after yesterday,' said Anna. 'What a crowd.'

Together they relived the thrill of the previous day's event, going through Anna's final clear round in minute detail. Then as they came down from the wooded hill on to the sandy foreshore Anna spoke quietly of her father's next ambition for her.

'He's entered me for the Western Counties' Championship at the beginning of September. It's sponsored by a cigarette firm and the first prize is three thousand pounds.'

'Anna!'

After that the girls could talk of nothing else and lingered on the seashore long after they had filled the bucket full of mussels. It was not until Mary remarked that the tide was coming in that Anna looked at her watch, and suddenly went pale.

'It's past lunch time. Daddy will be furious!'

Mr Dewar was waiting in the farmyard for Anna's return. He was wearing a smart tweed suit and his car was parked nearby. He stared straight through Mary and then spoke curtly to Anna.

'Get changed and get in the car. You'll have to do without lunch. You know we have to be in Plymouth this afternoon to buy your clothes.'

Mary stared at Anna in surprise that her friend had not mentioned such a big event. But Anna turned away and hurried into the house and, conscious that Mr Dewar was looking at her with some disapproval, Mary picked up the bucket full of mussels.

'I'll take these home and boil 'em and then share them out.'

'Do as you wish, Mary.'

'Why should Anna have gone all the way to Plymouth just to buy some clothes?' Mary said to her father later. 'Her mother usually takes her in to Silverstock.'

'You live *your* life, Mary,' replied Mr Wilkins tersely. 'And let Anna Dewar live hers.'

In the stable that evening, Mary heard the car come back. She saw Mr Dewar getting some dress-boxes out of the boot, with little frills of white tissue paper frothing out of them. She turned back to continue feeding September his oats, and then she heard Anna's footsteps coming across the cobbled yard towards the stable.

'Mary, there's something I haven't told you.'

Anna was leaning over the stable door, swinging slowly, her hair very fair in a slant of evening sunlight. Mary felt peculiar.

'I shan't be going back to Silverstock next week. I'm going away.'

'Going away?' repeated Mary inanely. She was stupefied with shock.

'To school. Daddy's sending me to Kilmingdean.'

That was the beginning of all the changes.

TWO

ANNA'S PROMISE

'Why does he want you to go to boarding school?' was all Mary could think of to say, her heart feeling like a stone within her. *'Why?'*

'Well, because of the riding, I suppose,' said Anna awkwardly.

She stopped swinging on the stable door now and came and stood beside Mary in the shadows, just in front of September's loose box. The horse looked up from his oats as she arrived and contentedly let her stroke his muzzle.

'The riding?'

'Well, yes. It's a big thing at Kilmingdean.'

Suddenly Mary realized that Anna was talking about one of the most famous girls' boarding schools in the West. She had read about it in the newspapers. The daughters of Heads of State had been there in the past and so had some of the country's leading women show-jumpers.

'You'll meet quite different sort of girls there, then?' Mary said, and she felt frightened. 'Different from—' she was going to say 'me' but changed it. 'Different from Silverstock School. Daughters of top families and all that. Your dad would like that for you?'

'Yes,' said Anna, with honesty. 'He wants me to mix with people from my own sort of background, now I'm growing up.'

Mary was silent.

14

'But it's the riding more than anything,' Anna said hastily. 'I should really have started after the summer holidays, that's the start of the new school year, but he's managed to get me in for the summer term. I don't know how he wangled it. The riding instruction is so fantastic there, you get about ten hours a week. He thinks it'll make all the difference to the Western Counties' Championship.'

'He must be dead set on you winning it.'

'He is.' Anna frowned, and sighed a little, like someone carrying a heavy burden. 'It seems terribly important to him, I can't quite understand it. I almost feel as though I'll let him down if I don't win it.'

'But that's silly,' Mary protested. 'With all that money to be won some of the top jumpers will be there. It would be just great if you could win it, but surely your dad doesn't *expect* . . .'

'*Anna!*'

Mary felt Anna's body stiffen beside her as Mr Dewar's voice rang out across the farmyard in the still evening air.

'Come and bring some of these boxes in. And your mother wants you to get tidied up. The Donaldsons are coming for dinner.'

Anna ran over to the stable door and leaned out.

'Just saying goodnight to September, Daddy.'

Then she ran lightly back to Mary's side and squeezed her hand warmly. Mary's loyalty over the Championship had touched her.

'Cheer up,' she said. 'I feel awful about keeping it from you, but Daddy's only been able to fix it up at the last minute. Let's have a proper talk—tomorrow. I've got the whole day free. Let's get a picnic and go down to the beach.'

'Okay.'

Anna went. Mary heard her footsteps echoing over the cobbles and then, a few seconds later, the sound of the farmhouse door shutting. Left alone with September in the shadowy stable, the tears began to roll down her cheeks.

'What do you think of it?' she whispered to him.

Sensing her misery, the horse nuzzled her. Mary put an arm round him and stroked his mane. She thought of waiting for the school bus at the end of the lane every morning on her own, and coming back on her own every evening. All the funny things that happened during the day—she would have no one to tell them to.

'She'll be gone for three whole months. She'll be riding other horses instead of you, September. Entering competitions down there—and we won't be able to share in them with her.'

In the comforting presence of the horse, Mary cried openly. Outside the orange sky darkened and dusk fell. At last she tip-toed home, under cover of darkness, and went straight up to her bedroom so that her father would not see that she had been crying.

The next day some of her feelings of foreboding, that nothing could ever be the same again, were dispelled. It was a beautiful day and both girls lived it to the full.

Mary was woken by April sunshine shafting in through her bedroom window and the sound of her father taking the cows down the lane after milking time. She got up and cooked him a big breakfast. When they had both eaten she did her jobs around the cottage and then took a bag of provisions across to the farm to make a picnic.

She let herself in through the back door of the farmhouse into the huge warm kitchen. Although she had never even seen the rest of the farmhouse she had always been allowed to come and wait for Anna in the kitchen, and she loved the big friendly room with its long old-fashioned cooking range, its gleaming copper pans and the oak beamed ceiling that was hung with onions, hams and every kind of fragrant herb.

She had just begun to butter some bread on the long pinewood table when Anna came in, crept up behind her and covered Mary's eyes with her hands.

'Snap!'

Mary wriggled round and then laughed. The two girls were identically dressed in blue denim jeans and white polo necked jumpers. Anna took the knife from Mary's hand.

'I'll make the picnic—you go and saddle up September.'

'You bet,' said Mary. She went across to the shelf by the door. 'Where's his hoof oil?'

'Not there?' Anna thought for a moment. 'I left it in the stable on Wednesday I think. Yes—I did. When we were getting ready for the gymkhana.'

Mary went to the stable, gave September a good feed, oiled his hooves and saddled him up.

'We're going out,' she told him. 'As if you didn't know!'

They set off sedately with the picnic in a knapsack, Anna mounted on September and Mary walking alongside. They skirted round the big field, where Mr Dewar was out sowing, conscious of his eyes upon them, and then up the track that led into the woods.

'Jump up!' giggled Anna, once they were amongst the trees, safely out of sight of the farm. 'Daddy can't see us now.'

It was some time since Mr Dewar had forbidden Anna to ride double saddle with her friend, complaining that it was unladylike and not particularly good for the horse. But September seemed positively to enjoy cantering with both girls on his long, strong back, and the friends liked getting around that way.

They rode through the woods over a bed of spring flowers, past sheep grazing amongst the trees, crested the hill and then rode down the other side, out of the sun-dappled woodland and on to the sandy shore.

The hours sped by in a blur of happy activity. They took it in turn to gallop September along the broad expanse of sand while the tide was out, jumping him over low piles of driftwood and small rocks. When the tide started to come in they tethered the horse by a grassy bank and then ran down to the water's edge and plunged in, letting the waves wash over them. They ate a huge lunch, basked in the sunshine sleepily, and then went off looking for shells.

All this time they avoided speaking about Anna's going.

As the afternoon wore on, it was Mary who finally spoke. She and Anna were seated on a slab of rock, sorting through their shells. Mary had found the prize, a huge white shell tinged with pink at the edges. She put it to her ear and could hear the sound of waves breaking.

'It's beautiful,' said Anna enviously. 'I wish I'd found it.'

'I found it for you,' said Mary simply, and handed it to her friend. She could not help the tears coming into her eyes. 'Have it. It's a present from me. I want you to take it away to school with you. If you put it to your ear sometimes, you'll hear the sea, and perhaps it'll remind you of all the good times we've had . . . down on this beach.'

As Mary's voice faltered Anna suddenly put an arm round her.

'Don't cry, Mary—*please* don't—you'll make me cry, too.'

'I can't help it. I've suddenly got this feeling again, I had it last night, that everything's going to change, that nothing will ever be the same again.'

'Of course everything's not going to change!' protested Anna. She looked straight into Mary's eyes. 'I won't be any different, just because I'm going away to school. I promise. You'll always be my best friend, Mary, nothing will ever change that.'

'You mean it?' asked Mary.

18

'Of course I mean it! Here—' Anna unfastened the clasp on the silver chain that hung round her neck. 'I want you to have this.'

'But it's your St Christopher, you always wear it!'

'I want you to have it, to keep. That's how much I think of you. Come on, let's put it on.'

Before Mary could stop her, Anna had fastened the chain round Mary's neck. Then she stood up and took Mary's hand to pull her to her feet. She pointed to September, grazing peacefully at the top of the sandy beach.

'And you'll have him, too, while I'm away,' she said softly. 'Will you look after him for me during term?'

'Of course I will!' said Mary joyfully. 'I'll feed him and groom him every day, and muck out the stable. And I'll see he gets plenty of exercise. Can I ride him, have you asked your father?'

'I'm sure you can. Daddy wants him kept in tip-top condition. He'll probably let you jump him sometimes as well.'

Suddenly Mary's heart was overflowing with something like happiness. She fingered the chain round her neck, as though for reassurance. Anna was going, but she would come back. She had sworn her friendship. She had entrusted her horse to Mary.

Nothing seemed as bad after that, even saying goodbye to Anna on Sunday, watching her climb into her father's car, a stranger in a mauve striped dress and mauve blazer trimmed with gold braid.

'I shan't be alone, after all,' she whispered to September when she picked out his hooves next morning. 'We've got each other. And, while we wait for Anna to come back, we're going to get you into really fine fettle. You've got a *very* important championship coming up in the summer holidays.'

The more Mary thought about it, the more of a privi-

19

lege it seemed to have been made responsible for September's well-being for the next three months. It gave her a new purpose in life.

But when she went across to the farmhouse to collect his hoof oil from the kitchen, she found the back door was locked. She had never known it to be locked before. She pulled at the bell for some time until the door was opened by Mr Dewar in person.

He stared at her for a moment without recognition.

Then he spoke irritably.

'Oh, it's you. What the dickens d'you want at this hour of the morning?'

THREE

SEPTEMBER MISBEHAVES

'I—I only wanted to oil September's hooves, sir,' stammered Mary.

'Where is it?' asked Mr Dewar tersely.

'On—on the shelf there,' said Mary pointing. It was clear that she was not expected to come in the kitchen and collect the hoof oil.

He fetched it and gave it to her.

'What's it in the kitchen for?'

'Well, Anna and I have always kept it in the warm, sir. Then it runs freely. We just always have, sir. I suppose it's silly.'

'Silly? It's ridiculous. Keep it in the stable with all the other stuff. Are you grooming him now?'

'Yes,' Mary nodded. 'That's why I'm up so early. You see, I go back to school today, so I thought I'd get it all done before breakfast.'

'I'll find my boots and come over,' said the farmer. 'I've been meaning to have a talk to you about the horse. I'd like to check everything's in order. Get back to work. I'll be over in a minute or two.'

Cheeks a little flushed, Mary obeyed.

'The kitchen door was shut, September,' she said to the horse. '*Locked*. What d'you think of that? And Anna's father has just told me to "get back to work". It's not really work, exactly, is it? Looking after you for Anna.'

The horse nuzzled her shoulder, sensing immediately that she was upset. Then he stood still and infinitely well-mannered, as always, as she polished his coat with a rubber to give it a sheen.

'Just finishing him off?' asked Mr Dewar as he came into the stable. He surveyed the grooming tools neatly set out on the shelf by September's loose box. 'Go easy with the body brush for a while. He needs to keep some grease on him while the days are still chilly—I'm planning to keep him out in the fields during the day while you're at school. Just use the dandy.'

He examined the horse's hooves, freshly picked out.

'I've done them, sir, I was just going to oil them.'

'They'll need picking out at least twice a day, so remember to do it when you get back from school. I'm also expecting you to look after his tack, Mary. I want the saddle and girths washed after they've been used, the leather kept soft—you've got some oil. We can't risk him getting sore or tender anywhere.'

'I've often done it for Anna,' Mary said promptly. 'And now I'll be riding him, I'll make sure the tack's kept in perfect condition.'

'I wanted to speak to you about that, Mary,' said Mr Dewar.

There was something in his tone of voice that made Mary uneasy.

'September is going to be out of competition work for three months now, until Anna comes home for the holidays. Of course you will ride him some days, for exercise, but his jumping's got to be kept up to scratch—improved upon, in fact.'

He broke off for a moment, a strange look in his eyes, and Mary knew that he was thinking about the Western Counties' Championship. Now she understood what Anna meant about it being so important to him, for his

22

body seemed to go tense as he thought about it.

'I realize that, sir. I was hoping that maybe I—'

'No.' He shook his head. 'No offence, Mary, but I can't take any chances with September. He's all we've got. I shall be jumping him myself, here on the farm, probably three or four times a week. You can help build the jumps, of course, and look after the horse and tack afterwards— but you must leave the jumping to me. Is that understood?'

Dumbly, Mary nodded. The last few minutes had begun to seem like a bad dream. But the final touch had yet to be added.

'I'm going to get my breakfast now, and you'd better get yours.'

He turned, ready to leave, his hand groping in his jacket pocket. Mary heard a rustling sound and then he was handing her something.

'Here's a pound to be going on with. You're going to have to work quite hard, so I've arranged with your father for you to be paid a small wage, two pounds a week. You'll get the other pound at the weekend, if you've proved you can do the job satisfactorily.'

'I—I—don't want—' Mary began, her face hot with indignation, her voice barely more than a whisper.

Mr Dewar was not even listening to her, for a strange thing happened then. He reached out his hand to touch September's muzzle and the horse went quite tense, drew back his head, and bared his teeth.

'What's the matter with you fellow?'

The farmer shrugged, went out through the stable door, and strode across the cobbled yard to the house, whistling loudly.

'I've—I've never known you be unfriendly to Mr Dewar before,' said Mary, gazing at September in surprise. She looked at the pound note in her hand, and her voice broke a little. 'It's almost as though you know how I'm feeling right now.'

He made a low whinnying sound in reply.

Mary hurried home to the cottage to cook her father's breakfast, barely able to contain her indignation. As soon as he came in through the door, she burst out at him:

'I was locked out of the farm this morning—I had to ring the bell. And Mr Dewar treated me like, well like a servant! It was horrible. He's going to *pay* me for looking after September. And I'm not to be allowed to jump him. Anna wanted me to jump him, I know she did—'

'Well, Anna's not the boss of Chestnut Farm, is she?' said John Wilkins shortly, washing his hands at the sink. He came and sat down, eating his porridge hungrily. As well as milking the herd this morning, he had had a sick calf to contend with and was not in the best of tempers. 'As for traipsing in and out of the farmhouse kitchen, well they're entitled to some privacy aren't they?'

'But they come in here.'

'That's different.'

'I've always been allowed to go in the kitchen.'

'That's because you were a child, you and Anna being playmates. But you're growing up now. Anna's been sent away to school, to make a young lady of her.'

'I don't want to be paid for looking after September!' Mary burst out. 'I promised Anna I would. I like doing it.'

'Look, Mary, I'm just an employee here,' said John Wilkins, feeling the need to spell it out. 'And you're my daughter. They need a groom for the horse—and the job's yours, you should be pleased. He only wanted to pay you a pound.'

Mary's father turned to his bacon and eggs and stabbed at it, looking quite pleased with himself.

'But I wasn't having that. It's hard work looking after a horse, the way he wants that one looked after. I said you

24

were worth two. Nice bit of bacon, this. You ought to be thanking your dad. Tidy sum to put away in your Post Office each week, eh? It'll mount up.'

Mary nodded, trying to look pleased, but still feeling humiliated.

'That horse has made them a fair bit already, and if it pulls off the Western Counties', well that'll be three thousand pounds for a start. Let alone all the money they can make getting Anna and September doing adverts and that. That's if they don't decide to sell the horse for a small fortune at the end of the season—'

'Surely they wouldn't do that?' asked Mary.

'No, I suppose not,' said her father. Then he muttered: 'But Mr Dewar isn't rolling in money these days, I know that for a fact. He's pinning a lot on to Anna's show-jumping. And if you're going to do half the work, I don't see why you should be made use of.'

'It's not like that at all,' Mary protested. 'Not with Anna.'

'No.' John Wilkins put his big weatherbeaten hand on his daughter's shoulder, speaking kindly now. 'I'm sure it's not. Not with the girl. Now you go and get yourself ready, you mustn't be missing the school bus. You'll be wanting to make yourself some new friends this term.'

Mary felt no desire to make friends. She sat alone on the seat that she had always shared with Anna, as the bus bumped along the country lanes that morning on its way to Silverstock. She sat and fingered the St Christopher on its chain that had always hung round Anna's neck, and it filled her with reassurance. *'You'll always be my best friend, Mary. Nothing will ever change that.'* The words echoed through her mind and filled her with happiness.

It was as a friend that Anna had asked her to care for September in her absence. The idea of her being a hired groom had been sorted out between their two fathers. If

Mr Dewar wanted to pay her two pounds a week, let him. She wouldn't let it make any difference. She would ignore it.

She would show all her affection for Anna by pouring out affection upon the horse, looking after his every need, making sure he did not pine for his mistress. She would write to Kilmingdean School as often as she possibly could, giving all the news of September in minute detail, for she knew that Anna must be missing him. Anna would write letters back. The time would soon pass.

Yet in the very first letter that Mary wrote to her friend, the news was not good, however much she wanted it to be.

'I'm afraid September is being a bit difficult with your father,' she wrote. 'We put jumps up in the water meadow, some quite straightforward ones, but he refused the brushwood fence twice and he even refused that old door we painted white before Easter. It's not a bit like him, is it? He's being perfectly all right with me, his old friendly self, though I know he's missing you. But I think the thing is he's not used to a man jumping him, and really your father's not had much to do with him up to now. I expect he'll be all right soon. I hope so. . . .'

It was only to September that Mary confided her innermost thoughts after that unhappy jumping session. She had taken his tack off in the stable and was rubbing him down before setting to work with the sweat scraper.

'You're in quite a lather. What got into you out there? You're being quite unfriendly with Mr Dewar. It's almost as though you *disapprove* of him or something. Do you think he's pushing you and Anna too hard? Is that it?'

Anna wrote back to Mary by return. The letter, on official school notepaper, with the Kilmingdean crest embossed on the back of the thick cream envelope, was the most impressive-looking thing that the postman had ever brought Mary Wilkins.

With trembling fingers she placed it unopened in her school satchel. It was too precious to read hurriedly over breakfast. She would save it for the long journey on the school bus.

FOUR

A RIVAL

'Postman brought you a letter then?' said John Wilkins over breakfast.

Mary bit her lower lip and said nothing. The envelope lying in her satchel was somehow so sacred to her she hadn't wanted her father to know about it. He must have met Tom, the postman, when he was taking the cows back up the lane after milking.

'From Anna is it then?'

Her father was in a good humour this morning; the little brown and white calf had completely recovered and not only the vet but Mr Dewar himself had warmly congratulated him on the way he had nursed her.

'Yes,' said Mary, trying to sound as casual as possible. 'Only I haven't even read it yet. I'll read it on the way to school.'

'Well, she hasn't forgotten you then,' said her father, munching his fried bread. 'Fancy writing already.'

'Why shouldn't she?' replied Mary with surprising force. 'Anna isn't going to change, I know she isn't.'

Her father said nothing, but gave her a knowing look which made her feel both angry and afraid. They finished the meal in silence and Mary was glad when he went out of the cottage to load up the milk churns.

She washed up the breakfast things and then hurried up the lane to catch the school bus. Settled comfortably in her seat by the window, oblivious of the babble of voices all around her and the jolting of the vehicle on the country road, she took the thick envelope out of her satchel and held it in her hand for several moments, just liking the feel of it. Then, taking the steel ruler from her geometry set, she carefully slit it open.

'Darling Mary, Your letter was like manna from heaven, I can tell you, I was feeling so homesick when it arrived. I still am. I'm missing September so much. How awful that he isn't getting on with Daddy, but I'm glad you told me —you must tell me everything—don't keep things back will you?

'I don't think it's just that he isn't used to Daddy taking him over jumps. I think Daddy's tense about September and me being good enough to win the Western Counties' and S. hates it when anyone's tense. He's such a sensitive old thing, do you remember when we first had him, and how funny he was until he got to know us?

'I know just how September feels because I'm feeling a bit tense myself about it all. I've thought about it a lot since I got here. I mean, Daddy sending me here in the middle of the school year like this—it was such a funny thing to do. (Oh, please don't show this letter to a soul, will you?) Of course, I know he did it for the riding, and that's fantastic. Miss Kilroy, my instructress here, is a genius—and an absolute slave-driver—she's spotted all sorts of tiny little faults that I'd never noticed, and I can feel my jumping improving already.

'What I mean is, I know coming here this term will help me a lot for the Western Counties', but why all the hurry? I could have started in the Autumn Term, when there'll be lots of other new girls, and entered for it *next year*. You've no idea how awful it is being the only new girl; everyone's settled with their own little group of friends and I feel completely left out in the cold. Of course, nearly all the girls

29

come from rich families and though I hate to say it, some of them seem awfully snobbish, talk about Hunt Balls all the time, and how they've met the Royal Family and all the rest of it.

'All in all, I feel a bit fed up with Daddy—don't breathe a word of this to anyone will you? I only hope I don't let him down after all this. I'm going to work really hard and the one bright spot is the horse I'm going to ride this term. If we get on well, Miss Kilroy is going to enter me for several events. His name is King of Prussia, and he really *looks* like a king, the most beautiful horse you ever saw, very regal—not a bit like darling old September! I'm going to ride him for the first time on Monday. Of course no horse can ever take September's place, I miss him so much I could cry. Tell him that, won't you?

'I do hope he'll settle down with Daddy soon. I was so hoping that Daddy would let *you* give him all the jumping he needs, somehow he's never quite cottoned on to the fact of how good you are, but there it is.

'I do miss the farm. I'm already counting the weeks till the end of term! I wonder if the thrushes have hatched yet in the hedge by your back door? I'm missing you, too. I put the shell to my ear last night, and I heard the waves as clear as anything. *Please* write again soon and give me every tiny scrap of news, especially about September!'

Mary read the letter through three times in all, savouring every sentence to the full. She was sorry that Anna was not settling down well at Kilmingdean so far—sorry, and yet —what a wonderful letter! It gave Mary the reassurance she longed for. Her father was wrong, and she was right! Anna hadn't forgotten her, anything but. She wasn't going to change and this letter proved it.

She put it carefully back in her satchel. Like the chain that hung around her neck, it would be another precious talisman to speed her through the weeks that lay ahead.

That weekend Mary was as happy as she had ever been. Chestnut Farm seemed to be bathed in permanent spring sunshine. She spent most of Saturday with September, cleaning out his stables, grooming him from head to foot, and then riding him in the woods which were blazing with wild flowers.

'Just look at the lambs, frolicking about among the trees!' she murmured to the horse. 'They're getting so big already.'

September seemed to sense Mary's new-found happiness that weekend and it put him in a calm frame of mind. At any rate when Mr Dewar spent an hour jumping with him on Sunday afternoon he performed quite well.

'Much more like his old self today,' said Mr Dewar afterwards, as Mary came across to take him back to the stable. 'Now he's ready to move on to bigger things.'

He handed Mary a pound note.

'Here's the rest of your wages for this week. You're doing a good job.'

She took the money in some embarrassment. She was still not reconciled to being paid for something that she regarded as a pleasure and privilege, but nothing could mar her happiness this weekend.

'Thank goodness you're settling down with him,' she told the horse, as she unsaddled him and prepared to feed him.

'I shall write to Anna tonight. She's going to be *very* pleased with you.'

By the time she had fed September, given him a thorough grooming and cleaned all the tack, it was time to cook supper for her father. Tired though she was, she found the energy to write Anna a long letter before she went to bed, full of news and tit-bits about the horse and the farm.

'P.S.' she put at the very end of the letter, 'the thrushes *have* hatched, I heard them cheeping below my window when I woke up this morning. Please write soon.'

During the next few days Mary learnt what Mr Dewar had meant about September moving on to bigger things. In their spare moments two of the farm hands were hard at work in the meadow, digging a huge ditch. On one side of the ditch they then constructed a high brushwood fence.

By Wednesday evening the work was finished. Mary went out into the meadow to bring in September who had been grazing there all day. She found Mr Dewar standing by the ditch speaking to Henry, one of the farm hands.

'It'll do for now,' he said, eyeing the ditch. 'Though I fancy we may have to widen it as time goes on. It's the same width as the Dyke now, but I won't be satisfied until September can jump something even wider. That way we take no chances when the big day comes.'

He came across and gave the horse a slight slap on its hind quarters.

'Take a good look at it old chap,' he said. 'It's Chestnut Farm's own Demon's Dyke—and we've built it specially for you. You're going to learn how to jump it—and jump it well.'

To Mary's eyes the jump looked rather terrifying and it seemed to her that the horse thought so too. Whether it was Mr Dewar's uncompromising tone of voice, or the sight of that wide ditch and high brushwood fence, September started moving his head around rather fretfully.

'What's the Demon's Dyke, sir?' she asked, at the same time patting the horse's neck to calm him down.

'It's where they all come unstuck at Imchester,' replied Anna's father tersely. 'Even the best show jumpers in the the country.'

Mary understood now. The Western Counties' Championship was always held at Imchester. She started to lead September away.

'One minute, Mary.'

'Yes, sir?'

'I'm at market all day tomorrow. I want to start him on this new jump as soon as possible, but it'll have to be Friday. When you get home from school get him all ready for jumping, will you?'

'On Friday? Yes, sir.'

Mary was gripped with uneasiness, but she tried to hide her feelings from the horse. In the stable, as she fed him, she said:

'I'm sure it's not half as difficult as it looks. *You* can do it, September, I know you can. Then we'll have some more good news to write to Anna won't we?'

At the mention of his mistress's name, September's ears seemed to prick up, and he looked round towards the stable door.

'No, she isn't here,' laughed Mary softly. 'She's still away. But she's here in spirit—and she wants to know everything you're doing.'

Mary got up eagerly the next morning, feeling sure that the postman would bring a reply to the letter she had posted to Anna on Monday morning. But nothing came. By Friday morning she was so convinced that there would be a letter from Anna that she went up the lane to meet Tom on his rounds.

'Sorry, love. Just some bills for Mr Dewar. Would you like to take them back for me?'

The letter came by second post and was waiting for Mary when she got back from school. She had the cottage to herself and slit the envelope open eagerly, using a knife from the kitchen drawer.

'Dear Mary, It was so good to get your letter—what a sport to write back so quickly when I was feeling low. You'll be glad to know I'm much more cheerful now, in fact I'm quite ashamed of that silly letter I wrote you. (Be a dear and tear it up.) First of all, King of Prussia

B   33

is quite the most fantastic horse—we seem to be made for each other. Even Miss Kilroy is delighted and that's saying something. And since I've been jumping him the girls here have really been sitting up and taking notice, and I've made one friend in particular—her name's Delphine (she's Judge ——'s daughter). You'll never believe this, but Del's family live in an old castle—a real one—near Oxford, and she's asked if I'd like to come and stay with them over half-term ! !'

The rest of the letter blurred in front of Mary's eyes. She looked in vain for the name that was so beloved and familiar, but it came only at the very end of the letter :

'What a joy that September is settling down with Daddy now. Give him a hug and a kiss from me, and tell him to keep up the good work.'

FIVE

HOPING AGAINST HOPE

'Put the kettle on, Mary!'

As her father banged on the back door and called out, Mary leapt up and hurried to fill the kettle, leaving the letter on the kitchen table. She could hear him scraping the mud off his boots outside.

'Another letter from Anna then?'

He had come into the kitchen before she could hide it.

'Yes,' said Mary, and put it in her pocket.

John Wilkins glanced at his daughter's face and said nothing.

'Mr Dewar's putting the horse over the big new jump this afternoon ain' he?' he said at last. He could sense that Mary was unhappy and was trying, in his own awkward way, to make conversation. 'You'll have work to do.'

'Yes.' Mary glanced at the kitchen clock. 'I've got to go over to the stable in about ten minutes and get September saddled up.'

'Just time to have a cup of tea and a sandwich, then, girlie . . .'

But Mary hardly heard him. September! Now that she had spoken the name out loud, tears began to well into her eyes and she had to fight to keep them back. She vowed to herself that she must hide her feelings from September; if he was to master 'Demon's Dyke' this afternoon, it was important that nothing should upset him.

35

In spite of her good intentions, the sight of him waiting for her at the meadow gate was too much for her. She opened the gate and led him out, in the direction of the stable. She tried to make her voice sound bright and cheerful but there was a little break in it that she simply could not control.

'Come on, boy. We've got to get you saddled up. You're going to do the big one today—the new jump.'

He knew at once that she was unhappy. As she saddled him up in the stable, he nudged her shoulder with his nose, and whinnied. After that Mary could not stop the words pouring out :

'You've got a rival, September. So have I. I don't know which is worse. I've had another letter from Anna today. Not a bit like the first one. I'm so miserable I could die. I was going to hide it from you, but what's the use? We can't hide anything from each other. She's starting to *forget* us, boy, both of us . . . I really do believe she is. We're in exactly the same boat, you and I.'

After that it was a relief to let the tears come and then rest her tear-stained cheek against September's silky coat, until some of the emotion had passed. All the time, he pawed the ground fretfully, as though he had understood every word.

'Mary !'

'J—just coming, sir.'

The sound of Mr Dewar's voice as he called to her to bring the horse out, brought something like panic to Mary's heart. What had she done?

'Oh, September,' she whispered, soothing him with her hand. 'I'm such an idiot behaving like this. You mustn't take any notice of me, you really mustn't. You've got big things to do out there. And I know you can succeed, I just *know* it.'

But from the moment Mr Dewar cantered the horse

36

round the meadow to loosen him up, Mary knew that it was going to be a bad session.

He took three or four hurdles carelessly, as though his heart wasn't in it. Then Mr Dewar headed him round in a tight circle towards the high brushwood fence that lay on the near side of the new jump. September took three or four strides towards it and then, as though changing his mind at the last moment, stopped dead.

He had balked.

'What's the matter with you, you brute!'

Mary winced as the farmer struck the horse hard with his crop, all his pent up tension and disappointment expressed in the blow. She felt as though she herself had been struck.

'Now take a note of that. You're going to do it, d'you hear?'

Then he shouted to Mary:

'Give Henry a hand. Take off the top layer of brush.'

Mary rushed forward and helped the farm hand carry away some of the brushwood. Now the jump did not look half as formidable and after very slight hesitation, September cleared the barrier easily. He was not expecting the wide ditch on the other side, however, and got across it with only inches to spare.

'That'll do for today,' said Mr Dewar, as he dismounted. He led the horse across to Mary. She noticed that there were beads of perspiration on Anna's father's forehead, quite out of proportion to the amount of riding he had done. 'I can see I'm going to have to take him into it gradually. I don't know what's the matter with the animal. A taste of the whip's the only thing he seems to understand today.'

As soon as they were alone together in the stable, Mary flung her arms round the horse's neck.

'Oh, you poor thing,' she whispered, her voice choked

37

with emotion. 'There was no need for that. I don't know what's the matter with *him*, these days. Fancy taking you straight into the fence at full height, anyway. He must have known you were unsettled today.'

It was some relief to Mary's guilty conscience to know that, even if September had been in a calm frame of mind to start with, Mr Dewar would soon have unsettled him today. Anna's father was obsessed with the Western Counties' Championship and was displaying an impatient and intolerant side of his character that she had never been aware of before.

She rubbed the horse down and thought : He's so highly strung. Things are communicated to him so easily. Mr Dewar's going to have to be much more relaxed than this. And I've got a responsibility, too. I mustn't show September when I'm feeling down. *I've got to try and hide it from him somehow.*

So it was that before she left him, she forced herself to be encouraging :

'You know something, September. That "Demon's Dyke" thing will never be as bad again. It's always worst the first time. You know what it's like now—you know all about that whopping ditch that lies on the other side of the barrier. All you've got to do is jump better and better until you can just curl up your lip and laugh at it.'

In her bedroom that night she sat down and wrote Anna a long account of how September had got on. Somehow it was second nature to confide everything to her, and hadn't she herself said in that first wonderful, letter : 'You must tell me everything—don't keep things back will you?'

In the cold light of morning, Mary remembered that Anna had said that before Delphine had come along, and before she had started to ride King of Prussia, the horse that looked so beautiful and regal, 'not a bit like darling old September'. She was undecided whether or not to post the letter and then she overheard a conversation between the Dewars which finally set her mind against it.

Mary had scarcely seen Mrs Dewar around the farm since Anna had left for Kilmingdean and she had guessed that she was missing her daughter a great deal. Once she had noticed her in the kitchen garden, a tall figure with hair very fair like Anna's but flecked with grey, wandering along the paths, stooping now and then to tend a plant, her shoulders hunched rather forlornly.

But she was out and about this Saturday morning. The sun had brought her out and in fact she had walked down the lane with her husband to the cow sheds, having decided to see the little brown and white calf that John Wilkins had nursed back to health.

They came into the dusky sheds and did not see Mary in the stall by the door, trying to find an overall that her father had mislaid. They were deep in conversation. Embarrassed, Mary stood silent in the shadows.

'We must write to Anna this weekend,' Mr Dewar was saying. 'But we had better not tell her how disappointing the horse's performance is lately. You know, Sarah, I'm beginning to wonder if the animal is past his best.'

'Surely not, Richard. He's not that old.'

'Some reach their peak early.'

There was a pause and then Mrs Dewar said in a bitter voice :

'I couldn't bear to think of such a thing. We have no hope of buying a better horse before the championship. It's been such a sacrifice, sending Anna to Kilmingdean— in more ways than one. If it were all in vain—'

'I've said all along it's a gamble, Sarah.'

'I couldn't bear to think of it all being in vain.'

Their footsteps echoed over the stone floor and then the subject was changed as they stopped in front of one of the stalls.

'There she is. Little Mirabelle. John was quite wonderful with her.'

'He's a man in a thousand. We're lucky to have him, Richard.'

Cheeks burning, Mary tip-toed out of the sheds and fled up the lane to Primrose Cottage. In her bedroom she read what she had written to Anna, a faithful account of how September had balked at the 'Demon's Dyke'. Now Mr Dewar's words were running through her head, over and over again:

'I'm beginning to wonder if the animal is past his best.'

To Mary such a thought was preposterous. But supposing, just supposing, Anna began to think along those lines —began, perhaps, to compare September directly with the 'fantastic' King of Prussia who so filled her thoughts at the moment?

She tore the letter into tiny pieces. She would not write a word to Anna until she had some really good news to report on September's progress: could describe his achievments in glowing terms, and thus remind her with which horse her affections—and her future—truly lay.

It was two whole weeks before Mary could write such a letter. At last, after much tribulation, and with a great deal of behind-the-scenes encouragement from Mary, September cleared the 'Demon's Dyke' with the brushwood fence at its full height, and cleared it magnificently. He went on to repeat the feat the same afternoon.

'Your father was very pleased, naturally,' wrote Mary. 'Now he is going to set the men on widening the ditch next week and make the jump even more difficult than the real Demon's Dyke. After that he's going to make a 'crowd' of us stand by the jump, because on the real course the Dyke is right on a corner, where all the spectators gather and there's a lot of noise. So you can see he's thought of everything. . . .'

Three weeks passed before Anna replied to Mary's letter. While briefly praising September ('tell him *jolly* good from me, won't you?') her letter was mainly devoted to detailed accounts of two local events she had entered on King of Prussia, and won. Delphine had come with her and been 'an absolute brick'. But it was the last paragraph that Mary stared at in disbelief:

'Half-term starts on Thursday and of course I'm going straight to Delphine's and—guess what—we've been invited to a Hunt Ball on Friday night. My godmother has sent me a beautiful dress to wear. As if that isn't fantastic enough, we shall probably meet you-know-who at the Ball, (that's right, royalty) . . . I can't tell you how far away Chestnut Farm seems these days, light years, I can tell you!'

From the drawer in her dressing-table Mary took that first letter Anna had written, about the snobbish girls at the school who talked about Hunt Balls and the Royal Family all the time. Surely the two letters had not been written by the same person! Then she fingered that other talisman, the St Christopher on its chain that hung always round her neck. What had Anna said? 'You'll always be my best friend, Mary, nothing will ever change that.'

A sudden thought struck Mary and all day it filled her heart with a curious lightness. When she fed September that evening she confided it:

'Anna *isn't* the same person. Kilmingdean has cast some horrible spell over her. And when she comes home in July, home here to Chestnut Farm, and sees us again—she'll come back to being herself. All the rest will be like a dream.'

From now on she would be hoping against hope on that.

SIX

FROM BAD TO WORSE

Spurred on by Mary's encouragement, September continued to jump 'Demon's Dyke' well for a week or so. Even when the ditch had been widened and a further six inches in height added to the brushwood barrier, he cleared it with ease, for a whole fortnight, as if to show Mr Dewar what a great show-jumper he really was.

'You'll have nothing to worry about when you go to Imchester in (and on!) September,' Mary had written jubilantly to Anna at this time. 'Your father says some of the best show-jumpers in the country have come unstuck at the Demon's Dyke there, but *our* Demon's Dyke is now quite a bit more difficult, and September treats it like child's play.'

Anna had not replied for ages and her letter when it came was only a few lines long. Her life was such a whirl of activity these days, and her thoughts so bound up with King of Prussia whom she was taking to a show almost every week, that it was obvious that Chestnut Farm was still 'light years' away. Mary refused to let it hurt. She was living for the day when Anna came home for the summer holidays, home to Chestnut Farm, and would be her old self once again.

Besides, the letter was so brief that it scarcely called for a reply, and as it turned out Mary would have been at a loss to know what to write to Anna after that.

She had long ceased to feel jubilant about September's jumping. After clearing 'Demon's Dyke' so well for a fortnight, the horse made a bad landing one afternoon when the far bank of the ditch was unusually muddy and slippery after heavy rains. If the bank had been firm he would have got away with it, but on this occasion he slithered back several feet, and threshed about wildly for some moments before he was able to regain his balance.

It was obvious to Mary that the incident had unnerved September for the time being and she ran forward to take his leading rein, fully expecting Mr Dewar to instruct her to take him away and rub him down.

'It's all right, Mary,' Mr Dewar said curtly. The lines of tension, which had not been so apparent lately, had returned to his face. 'He's not going in yet.'

He cantered September once round the field and then turned his head towards 'Demon's Dyke' and shouted :

'Come on, fellow, over it properly this time !'

Mary could hardly bear to look as September broke into a gallop and then, realizing where they were heading, skidded to a halt just a few feet away from the high brushwood barrier.

For Mr Dewar was hitting him with the riding crop now. Once, twice, three times—hard blows all of them— and his face was contorted with anger.

'Over, you stubborn beast ! Over !'

As the third blow struck his flank, September suddenly reared up on his hind legs, whinnying, so that Mr Dewar was thrown clean off his back. Then he bolted towards the gate.

Mary was there before him. Fearlessly she threw herself forward, one arm round his neck, seizing his rein with her other hand.

'Stop, boy. Stop. Calm down !'

He dragged her a few feet and then slowed down to a

43

standstill as she spoke softly, soothingly, all the time stroking his coat, stroking the fears away.

'It's all right, boy, it's me, Mary. Calm down, now, that's right . . . nice and calm . . . everything's okay.'

He stood perfectly still at the edge of the farm yard now, breathing heavily, reassured by her presence. She gently soothed his flank where the crop had stung him and there were tears in her eyes.

'He didn't mean to hurt you, September. He lost control of himself. This Championship is so important to him—it's all daft isn't it? Everything will be all right when Anna comes home. Just a few more weeks. You've just got to try and do your best till then, don't let him upset you.'

She watched as Mr Dewar walked slowly this way, none the worse for his fall, although his clothes were covered in mud. She did not attempt to take the horse to him.

'I think he's had enough for today, sir,' she blurted out. 'When he slipped on the bank, it unnerved him a bit, I could tell. That's why I came to get him—'

'I had to try him again,' said Mr Dewar curtly. He was quite calm again now, perhaps even regretting his display of temper. 'The quickest way for him to get his nerve back was to take him back over the jump straight away. I don't wish to be unkind, Mary, but you are hardly an expert on these things.'

Mary was silent. She would like to have said to Mr Dewar: I *am* an expert on September. Anna and I both know him better than you do. He's much too intelligent to become scared of a jump just because of one bad landing. He just needed time to get over it, that's all. Now you really *might* have put him off the jump—for good.

She would have liked to have said all that, but of course she did not dare. Instead she said politely:

'Shall I take him in now?'

'Yes please, Mary.'

44

As she rubbed the horse down she said to him:

'You will do the jump again, won't you, September? Tomorrow perhaps or the next day? You won't let this put you off? You mustn't.'

September did not seem to respond to her words. A fear gripped Mary and it grew larger every moment. Supposing from now on the horse refused to jump Demon's Dyke for Mr Dewar ever again?

She knew what she must do.

After her father had gone to bed that night, and the last of the farmhouse lights had been turned out, she crept downstairs from her bedroom, still fully clothed, and let herself silently out of the cottage. She tip-toed across the cobbles when she reached the farm yard and opened the stable door.

There was a good moon and a shaft of light illuminated September's loose box. Gently she roused the horse, a strange feeling of exhilaration coursing through her.

'It's me, boy,' she whispered.

As they cantered out to the meadow five minutes later, she glanced back towards the farmhouse, scared that at any moment the lights would come on and the door be flung open. But all was dark and silent beneath the deep Devon thatch of Chestnut Farm.

Seated firmly on September's back she bent and carefully opened the gate into the water meadow. The grass was heavy with dew and the moonlight made it shimmer beneath the horse's hooves as they cantered round in a circle.

'First a couple of easy ones—and then the big one, boy!' Mary said softly. 'After that, this afternoon will seem just like a bad dream.'

She was trembling a little. What a row there would be if this should ever get to Mr Dewar's ears. She had been strictly forbidden to jump on September while he

45

was in training for the Western Counties'!

But at that moment only one thing mattered—that September should get his confidence back. Because if he didn't, Mr Dewar might not want him any more. Ever since the horse had thrown Anna's father that afternoon, Mary had been haunted by the words she had heard spoken between Anna's parents that day: 'You know, Sarah, I'm beginning to wonder if the animal is past his best.'

First they jumped a low hurdle. Mary's hand shook a little as she held the rein, but now it was excitement that was making her tremble. It was so long since she and September had jumped together! It had always been fun, but tonight it was suddenly thrilling. September seemed to sense her excitement and joy, and both horse and rider were in perfect harmony. The weeks since Anna had gone away had brought them closer together—and now it was as if September had never been ridden by anyone else.

'The door—let's take the door next.'

Up and over the old white-painted door, sailing through the air as though they had jumped together every day all summer!

'Now for the Dyke!' laughed Mary, riding the horse round in a sweeping arc towards the high brushwood fence. It was bigger and more formidable than anything she had ever tackled in her life, but as the breeze whipped up her brown hair and lightly stung her cheeks, she was laughing out loud with exhilaration. 'I know we can do it, boy, and so do you. You're enjoying this every bit as much as I am!'

Up, up, up and over. As the horse cleared the barrier with inches to spare and flew over the ditch beyond, Mary closed her eyes tightly, just for a moment, in deep pleasure. It was pleasure that was tinged with longing.

As they landed lightly, she spoke from the bottom of her heart.

'Oh, September, September—I wish you were *mine*.'

46

Later, lying in bed in her small room, Mary felt ashamed of that moment of deep longing. It was wrong of her to want something that belonged to somebody else. September was Anna's horse.

When Mr Dewar next took September out, it seemed that Mary's plan had succeeded perfectly. He took Demon's Dyke twice, in faultless style.

It was in the days that followed that his behaviour became completely erratic. At one time he would clear the jump with ease and at other times he would shy right away from it. Some days he would sail over Demon's Dyke, even when Mr Dewar collected neighbours and farm workers together to stand in a small group right by it, chattering and cheering loudly to simulate the conditions that the horse would meet on the real course. Then, having done that, he would wilfully refuse a perfectly simple hurdle, as though he deliberately wanted to humiliate Anna's father.

Mr Dewar began to use the crop with increasing frequency, in his impatience and anger, but that did nothing to solve the problem. Mary was quite sure that she knew the reason for September's erratic form. The horse had come to hate Anna's father.

The fact that things had gone badly wrong between the farmer and his daughter's horse, seemed to have consequences of great magnitude. Mary could not understand it. Chestnut Farm had always been a happy place, and Mr Dewar had always been liked and respected by the men who worked for him. But during this period he seemed permanently irritable and continually found fault. One night Mary heard him having words with her father about the milk yield of the cows, and both men's voices were raised in anger, a thing she had never known before.

More than once she saw Mr and Mrs Dewar sitting on the rustic seat outside the farmhouse door watching the sun set behind the woods they owned on the hill, just staring

47

into space without speaking to one another. It was a melancholy sight.

More affected than anyone by the air of gloom, and secretly fearing for September's future, Mary could not bring herself to write to Anna. Anna did not write to her again, and so their letters ceased.

June was a very still month and there was a peculiar stillness about the farm as though they were all waiting for something. Then suddenly, towards the middle of July, the air of gloom lifted. Mary realized that she was not alone in pinning so much on Anna's homecoming. Only Anna could make everything come right.

SEVEN

THE HOMECOMING

As the days went by in July, Mary's heart became a little lighter each morning. The atmosphere on the farm was becoming gradually more cheerful.

'Even you can sense it, can't you, boy?' said Mary as she groomed September one morning. 'You've never forgotten her, have you, even for a day? You know Anna will be riding you again soon, and your days of training with Mr Dewar will be finished with for the time being.'

At the very name 'Anna', the horse looked eagerly about him as he so often did when he heard her mentioned. It was true that he sensed that she would soon be home and he certainly sensed the lightening of the atmosphere. How else could it be explained that for the past week his jumping had been so much less erratic. He had even earned some words of praise from Mr Dewar the previous day.

'We shall be able to give a good report of you when we see your mistress on Saturday,' he had said to the horse, almost jovially, as Mary came up to lead him away. 'Two clear rounds this afternoon, and good times as well. It'll be some good news after all the bad news we've been giving her.'

Naturally Mary had not been happy at that last remark. She had refrained from writing to Anna all this time, but it seemed that Mr Dewar had been sending through

49

bad reports on September's behaviour anyway. Had his letters turned her off the horse, made her compare September directly with her beloved King of Prussia? She should have realized that Mr Dewar would not be silent.

'Thank goodness you did so well today,' she had said to September afterwards. 'And I don't suppose Mr Dewar will take you round again before the weekend now. You are an extraordinary animal. It's almost as though you *know* that he and Mrs Dewar are going to see Anna.'

This weekend, the last weekend before the school broke up, Anna's parents were going down to Kilmingdean for three days and staying at a hotel. It was the school's Open Day on the Saturday but the real purpose of their visit was to stay until the Monday and watch the West of England Show events, nearby.

Miss Kilroy had persuaded the headmistress to allow Anna to enter for the Imperial Trophy show-jumping event on King of Prussia. Such an honour had never been bestowed on a Kilmingdean girl of Anna's age before.

'She can work miracles with that horse,' Anna's riding instructor had explained. 'I believe she can win the Imperial Trophy. She'll certainly not disgrace us. If ever a horse and rider were made for each other, it's those two. In fact there is a thought in my mind, Miss Jansen, that I would like to talk to you about.'

Miss Kilroy then went on to discuss with Miss Jansen, as she had in the past, her belief that King of Prussia had been an expensive mistake as far as Kilmingdean School was concerned. They had bought him for prestige reasons, a pure thoroughbred with a famous sire, for some of the best riders in the school to ride in competitions. As well as bringing honour to the school it had been felt that it would give a great deal of confidence to several girls if they could win important trophies on such a horse.

It had not worked out. King of Prussia, like many fine

show-jumpers who were also thoroughbreds, did not settle easily with different riders. He was a horse who, once he had found the rider of his choice, was restive and difficult with most others.

'Now he has found Anna Dewar. Frankly they are made for each other, and it is a joy to see them. But—'

'But we cannot really afford to maintain an expensive horse for one girl's benefit?' interposed the headmistress. 'Is that what you were about to say?'

'Exactly. We are taking a risk entering Anna for a difficult senior event but I believe she'll emerge with great credit. Furthermore, I feel certain that her parents, once they see them together in the Imperial Trophy, and faced with the prospect of Anna being separated from King through the long summer holidays, may well be prepared to make us a handsome offer for the horse.'

'Yes, yes, bound to,' said Miss Jansen. 'What parents wouldn't? Especially when you explain the situation to them. They will most likely leap at the chance, and the matter will be resolved happily from everyone's point of view.'

'Especially Anna's!' smiled Miss Kilroy. 'She adores that horse.'

So it was decided that Anna should enter for the Imperial Trophy.

On Monday evening Mary was in the stable later than usual, settling September down for the night. As soon as she heard the car pull up in the farm yard, doors slamming, Mr Dewar's voice full of cheerfulness and jubilation, she knew that something exceptional had happened.

She peered out of the stable door.

'Go and ring the Donaldsons to come over—Jack and Mary, too—'

'But Richard, we've been away since Saturday, I feel so disorganized!'

51

'Not too disorganized for some champagne, surely, Sarah! We're going to celebrate! We shall drink champagne—out of this!'

He was holding a huge silver cup in his hands.

As Mary realized that Anna had won the Imperial Trophy on King of Prussia, her heart gave a painful lurch and instinctively she glanced back towards September's loose box. She felt frightened for him.

Mary had no inkling of the conversations that had taken place so recently at Kilmingdean School, but she had always seen King of Prussia as a threat to September. She had never dared to think just how the threat might materialize, it was enough to know it was there.

Yet even as she looked at that silver cup, even as her fears for September's future reached their highest pitch, her mind was to be put at rest. For Mr and Mrs Dewar stood by the car talking for a few moments longer, and as their words carried across the still evening air, she found herself trembling with relief.

'Oh, Richard, didn't they look wonderful together? If only we could have accepted Miss Jansen's offer—'

'That's the tenth time you've said that, Sarah.'

'I'm sorry, dear. I did admire you—you carried it off so well. As though naturally we could afford to buy King of Prussia for Anna, and how kind of the school to offer, but we wouldn't dream of replacing September . . .'

'I couldn't let Anna down, could I? I mean, if you send a girl to Kilmingdean, it's taken for granted that you're rich, money no object. I had to pretend, even if it was only for Anna's sake.'

'It wasn't a mistake sending her to Kilmingdean, Richard?'

'You're always saying that, Sarah. Mistake! How can you talk about mistakes when we've brought home this.' He flourished the cup again, his voice rising in jubilation.

'Look how much the school's taught her already. This is only the beginning. Anna will make our old nag look like the most expensive show-jumper in Britain when she takes him to Imchester. Mark my words.'

'Of course, of course.' Mrs Dewar's voice was lighter now. 'If I'm going to get people round this evening, I'd better start 'phoning.'

Feeling weak at the knees, Mary tip-toed over to September and flung her arms round his neck. The words had been like music to her ears.

'Everything's all right, September,' she whispered. 'It really is. You're still Anna's horse and you always will be. They won't be sending you away from Chestnut Farm—they can't. And once Anna's been home a few days, everything will be just like it always was!'

In the week that Anna was due home, Mr Dewar took September round the jumps only once more. It could not have been a happier occasion. September, knowing that Mary was happy, and that his mistress was returning at any moment, was tranquil and eager to please. His rider, too, was more relaxed and good-humoured than Mary had seen him all summer. Now that Anna had won the Imperial Trophy, Mr Dewar's hopes for her winning the Western Counties' Championship had returned in full flood.

'Well, what did you think of him, Mary?' he asked afterwards, as she took September's rein. 'That last round, eh?'

It took Mary a moment or two to recover from the shock of being spoken to almost as an equal by Anna's father.

'Wonderful, sir. The best ever.'

'No more school, Mary?'

'We broke up today.'

'That's splendid. Because you've got a lot of work to do in the morning. Anna gets home after lunch. And when

53

she arrives I want this horse to be the first thing she sees. And I want you to groom him as if you were preparing him for a show. The full treatment in the morning, Mary.'

Mary nodded. That was exactly what she had been planning on herself.

By lunch time the next day, Mary was exhausted but happy. She had never given September a grooming like it. After washing him from head to toe in warm soapy water she had plaited his mane and pulled his tail. She had brushed his coat until it shone, picked out his hooves and oiled them, and then put a touch of grease round his eyes for added lustre.

'You look like a fashion plate, September,' she giggled excitedly. 'Anna will hardly recognize you!'

The horse seemed as excited as she was.

While she was having lunch with her father, she heard the Dewars' car go off to the station to meet Anna's train.

Now that the moment had almost arrived, Mary felt quite tense.

'You're not eating your lunch, girl,' observed John Wilkins. 'You must be hungry after all your hard work this morning.'

'I am hungry, Dad, but I just can't eat.'

'That's plain daft,' he said, giving her an uneasy glance. 'The whole place seems to have gone mad lately, just because Anna's coming home.'

'I know, Dad. It's been miserable while she's been away, that's why. Everything's going to be all right again now.'

'I hope you're right, Mary,' her father said gruffly. 'I only hope you're right.'

At any other time, her father's pessimistic tone would have cast Mary down at once. But today nothing could touch her. Anna must be stepping off the train just about now. Her father would load her suitcase into the boot of his car, a few minutes' drive from Silverstock and she would be here!

After the meal Mary just had time to give September's tack one last shine with the leather and then she saddled him up. Slowly she led him out of the stable into the farm yard, step by step, full of pride as she looked at him. He was holding his head beautifully, his coat was shining, he was a picture of health. She heard the car's engine, growing louder as it came down the lane, and then the car came bumping into the farmyard. It braked abruptly outside the farmhouse.

A shiver ran through Mary as she saw the familiar figure, sitting in the front seat next to her father. She saw the mauve blazer with gold braid, the fair hair a little longer than she remembered. September seemed to want to gallop forward; Mary had to restrain him.

'Yes, she's home, boy, Anna's home. But whoa back, slowly does it.'

They continued forward, across the farm yard, step by step. The horse's hooves rang out loudly on the cobbles. At any moment Anna must surely look this way and see them. Why didn't she look? Why were the three of them just sitting in the car, talking amongst themselves?

Mary could restrain herself no longer. Was the spell of Kilmingdean still clinging to her friend? Now surely was the moment when it could be broken. Here was September in the flesh, looking so beautiful, waiting to see his mistress again, as he had waited all these weeks.

'Anna!' she cried. 'Welcome home, Anna!'

The eager cry fell upon deaf ears. Anna was too busy quarrelling with her father. Furthermore, she was in floods of tears.

EIGHT

DISASTER

As she realized that Anna was crying, all Mary's excitement slipped away. She stood frozen to the spot, clutching September's mane. The horse obediently came to a halt, no longer straining eagerly forward to see his mistress. He, too, sensed there was something wrong.

'Miss Jensen offered us King of Prussia! She *offered* him to us! Why did you refuse to buy him, Daddy? Why?'

'Calm down, child, calm down.'

On this hot July afternoon the car windows were wide open and Mary could hear every word that the Dewars were saying, although Anna, her shoulders heaving, was completely unaware that Mary and September were only a few feet away.

'I could have had King for my very own—for always! I could have had him at school every term time and brought him home in the holidays. I know he would have cost a lot of money—'

'A very great deal of money, Anna. Especially when you consider you already have a fine horse—'

'September's gone off! You wrote and told me so! King would soon have paid for himself. You want me to win the Western Counties', don't you—?' Anna's voice was rising higher, she sounded almost hysterical. 'Well, I'd have won it on King! Now the school's decided he's got to be sold anyway. If not to us, then to somebody else.'

Anna's sobs broke out afresh and she buried her face in her hands.

'Do you realize he won't be there when I get back next term? That I'll never, never see him again?'

As Anna's mother leant forward to touch her daughter's hair and comfort her, Mr Dewar glanced round for the first time.

As soon as Anna had grown calmer he said sternly:

'Mary has brought September to see you. Don't you think you should get out of the car and say hello to them?'

Anna lifted a tear-stained face. Slowly she turned and gazed past her father to where Mary and September stood in the farm yard, as though only dimly recognizing them and remembering who they were. Mr Dewar got out of the car, went round and opened the passenger door and helped Anna out.

Gripping her arm he brought her round to this side of the car. She took two or three steps forward towards Mary. For an instant, September perked up.

'H-hello, Mary.'

She tried to form her lips into a smile, but they kept trembling.

'Hello, Anna,' began Mary, in a very small voice. 'I— I—'

Before she could think what to say Anna's face suddenly seemed to crumple. With a violent jerk, she pulled away from her father, turned and ran towards the house.

'Come back, Anna! Come back *at once!*' cried Mr Dewar.

Anna did not seem to hear. Blindly she raced towards the front door, which was slightly open, and disappeared into the house. Her mother got out of the car and hurried after her, looking forlorn and anxious.

Mary clung very tightly to September. His head was

57

hanging now in utter dejection. If it were possible for a horse to cry, then at that moment September would indeed have been crying.

Mary was so concerned about him that she did not notice Mr Dewar until he was right beside her.

'I'm sorry about this, Mary.' He glanced towards the house, his face pale and tense. 'You've gone to a lot of trouble with the horse. I'm afraid Anna is in a very emotional state at the moment, but she'll get over it, you'll see. You'd better unsaddle him and put him out to grass for the rest of the day.'

'Yes, sir.'

As Mary turned September's head round and led him away, Mr Dewar called:

'I want him saddled up for nine o'clock in the morning. Anna will be taking him over the jumps, I'll see to it that she does. She'll have recovered by then.'

In the stable Mary hung up the horse's tack. She could hardly bear to look at him. His eyes had grown dull, his movements were listless, and even his shining coat seemed to have lost some of its lustre.

'Oh, September.' She put her arms around his neck. 'Anna may have recovered by the morning—but will you? I don't think so, somehow.'

All her old forebodings about September, and his future here at Chestnut Farm, had returned with full force.

As the day wore on, and she was busy about the farm helping her father, she began to feel hurt for herself, as well as September. Not once did Anna emerge from the farmhouse or make any attempt to find her and speak to her. Mary had looked forward to this day for so long, ringed it in red in her diary! The day of Anna's return— the day when she could begin to forget about Kilmingdean School and start to think about Chestnut Farm again! The day when, so Mary had fondly imagined, a forgotten

58

friendship would be remembered and then gradually renewed.

When she went to bed that night, Mary took off the St Christopher on its chain and placed it on her chest of drawers. Somehow she did not want to wear it any more for the time being.

Promptly at nine o'clock the next morning, she led September out to the meadow, saddled up and ready for work. As Mr Dewar had forecast, Anna was out there, ready and waiting. Although Mary could tell from the dark rings under her eyes that she had probably been crying a great deal through the night, she had all the outward appearances of someone who had indeed 'recovered'. With her long fair hair brushed and gleaming in the morning sunlight and her figure trim in riding jacket and jodhpurs she was a picture of composure.

She was standing with her father and a family friend, surveying the jumps with an experienced eye. As Mary led September through the gate she immediately left her father's side and came across.

'Mary,' she said. 'It's wonderful to see you again.'

Mary stared.

'What's the matter, aren't you pleased to see me?'

'I—er—yes, of course, Anna,' Mary said. But inwardly she felt a cold hand about her heart. Anna was different! Her smile was different, a bit artificial somehow. And her voice! She hadn't noticed yesterday, but even that had changed. The soft Devonshire accent had almost disappeared.

It's the spell of Kilmingdean, and it's certainly not going, Mary thought with something like panic. *It's even worse than I thought.*

Thus, after the first shock, Mary could not feel any further shock at Anna's next words, spoken in loud carrying tones:

59

'I must say I'm thrilled to bits that Daddy's been paying you a small wage while I've been away. I've never seen September in such good nick, darling. As a matter of fact my friend Delphine's got a full-time groom for *her* horses but I've told her he's not a patch on *you*.'

As Anna rattled on, Mary saw that Mr Dewar was glancing towards them with approval. It was as though he were relieved and delighted that at last his daughter was being sensible in her attitude to his cow man's daughter.

'And how *are* you, old chap?' Anna was saying, some genuine affection creeping into her voice. She reached out to touch September's muzzle but he drew his head back and gazed at Mary with big mournful eyes, as if to say: *This isn't the Anna I remember.*

She took his rein but he was reluctant to move away from Mary.

'Go with Anna,' Mary said, in a tiny little voice. 'Go with her.'

After the first hesitation, September was totally obedient to Anna. He allowed her to mount him. When she commanded him to walk round the field, he walked. When she commanded him to canter, he cantered.

This was the girl who had schooled him, after all. This was his mistress. Sad and dispirited he might be, but the habit of years of being obedient and loyal to his mistress was deeply ingrained, even though he knew that her feelings towards him had changed.

Mr Dewar watched his daughter and the horse with growing pleasure. He did not notice September's lack of spirit, only the blind obedience.

'You can still do anything with him, just as you always could!' he called out. 'Start a few low jumps now. Build him up to the big one.'

As Mary watched September going over those preliminary jumps, she knew that all her fears were justified. His performance was ordinary and no more; it lacked all zest and sparkle.

'Once more round the field, and then the big one : The Demon's Dyke!' There was a shake of excitement in his voice. He had waited for this moment for so long. He was in a fever of impatience to see his daughter do the difficult jump that he had so often rehearsed with September : do it with all the new-found skill and finesse that she had learnt at her expensive school. 'Come on, Anna. Why are you slowing down?'

'I don't feel he can do it yet!' shouted Anna. 'Not this morning. It's just a feeling I have—'

'Of course he can do it!' yelled Mr Dewar, suddenly exploding with anger. 'What do you think I've been working so hard on all these weeks. He can do it easily, and that's with *me* in the saddle. Now he's got you.'

'No, Daddy, I know he can't—' Anna's thin layer of composure was cracking apart. Her voice was edgy and tearful.

Mary stood there in silence, not daring to speak, but willing with all her heart that Mr Dewar would listen to his daughter. How could he be so stupid as to ignore what she was saying!

Yet her words seemed to goad him from anger into fury.

'Get a grip on yourself, Anna! Stop talking such non-sense. Don't you realize Uncle Michael here has come twenty miles to see you do this. *Do it, I say! Take him over!*'

Pale and frightened, Anna cantered September round in a semi-circle and then headed him for the high brush-wood fence with the huge ditch beyond it.

'Come on, boy, you've got to jump it. I'm telling you. Come on—'

As Mary watched September gather speed she knew that nothing could stop him now. Anna had given her order and he would not disobey her. She also knew that this morning the animal had a heaviness and a weariness about him that made such a jump impossible. He would try but—

'September!' she screamed, as his front legs caught the top of the heavy brushwood. He was plunging down, down, into the ugly ditch with his right foreleg caught up awkwardly beneath his body.

'September!' she gasped, running hard until she came to the ditch.

He was lying there, unable to get up. Anna had been thrown clear. She staggered to her feet, bruised but otherwise intact.

'September's hurt!' cried Mary, the tears running down her cheeks.

Within seconds Mr Dewar was on his knees beside the animal.

'Run and 'phone the vet!' he shouted to his friend Michael.

Together he and Mary and Anna got September to his feet. But the horse was holding his right fore hoof off the ground.

'He's lame, Daddy!' said Anna, in distress. 'September's lame.'

'The Western Counties',' was all Mr Dewar could say. 'The Western Counties'.' He said it four times in all, and his face was ashen.

NINE

DEATH SENTENCE

They got September to the stable, limping badly, and Mary made his loose box comfortable with fresh straw, so that he could lie down until the vet arrived. There was a wound beneath the knee and a great deal of swelling of the leg.

Mr Dewar, his friend Michael and Anna waited by the horse for the vet to arrive. After a while Mrs Dewar came across from the farmhouse with mugs of coffee and waited with them. They all looked drawn and anxious and spoke little. No one noticed Mary, who pretended to busy herself by washing down the saddlery with leather soap in a corner of the stable, although having done it the previous day it did not really need doing again.

She tried to make herself as inconspicuous as possible. She could not bear it if she were sent away. She *had* to be there when the vet arrived, to know at once how things were for September.

At last Mr Peters arrived, with his big leather bag. He entered the loose box and knelt beside the animal, saying nothing for several minutes as he worked, treating the wound with penicillin and then applying poultices to the swollen flesh. All this time September was in pain, but he lay still and obedient.

'A good animal,' said Mr Peters at last, getting to his feet.

He started to pack his bag. Across the stable, Mary kept all thought and feeling suspended, even her very breath seemed to stop coming as she waited to hear his verdict.

Mr Dewar, too, for different reasons, was in an agony of suspense.

'Is his knee broken, Peters?' he rasped out at last.

'No.'

'It's not?' the relief rushed out of Mr Dewar. The questions poured out. 'Will he be all right then? He's entered for the Western Counties—let me see—September 14th— nearly eight weeks' time. Anna's riding him. It's very important to us. Is he going to make it?'

Mr Peters gave the farmer a peculiar look.

'I doubt it,' he said shortly.

'Why?' demanded Mr Dewar, in anger and disbelief.

'Let's put it this way, you certainly couldn't bank on it. I've known a horse with a sprain as bad as this recover completely, with weeks of rest and careful nursing. But that's unusual. I'm inclined to think he might have lost some joint oil. Even if he hasn't, the odds are that when he's recovered he'll never be fit for really hard work again.'

'You mean his show-jumping days are over?' asked Mrs Dewar, stunned.

'I can't be as definite as that,' said the vet, addressing Anna's mother more gently than he had her father. 'You can never tell with something like this. Those are the indications at present. He must be rested for a month, with the gentlest of exercise. The leg must be poulticed three times a day. When the swelling has gone down, the leg must be strapped up to give it firm support. Only then can we begin to tell if there's any hope of his returning to show-jumping.'

As the vet left, Anna fell on her knees beside September.

'Oh, you poor thing,' she sobbed. 'You poor, poor thing.'

Standing in the shadows, with the leather soap still in

her hand the tears began to trickle down Mary's cheeks, too. For a moment she felt close to Anna again. It gave her comfort, even hope, to know that the girl who had once been her best friend, who had returned from Kilmingdean a stranger, could weep like that. Surely she must still be the same Anna underneath?

At that moment Mr Dewar, who had seen the vet to his car, came back into the stable. His friend Michael was no longer with him. Seeing her husband alone, and forgetting Mary's presence in the stable, Mrs Dewar suddenly released all her pent-up emotion.

'You're a fool, Richard! I heard what you did out there! You made Anna take the horse over that jump before he was ready! This is all your fault!'

'What do you mean "before he was ready"?' snapped Mr Dewar. 'I've been training him for weeks. He could have jumped it if he wanted to: look at the times he's done it! The animal's a rogue, I tell you. He's become completely unreliable this summer, and that's all there is to it.'

As Mr Dewar paused for breath Mary, hot with embarrassment, noisily shifted the saddle to another place, anxious to remind the family of her presence. But they were too heated and upset to notice or care.

'He's only been erratic because Anna had gone away. She's back now. If only you'd given him a day or two to get used to her again—'

'This is all nonsense, Sarah. September's been a fine jumper in his time, after all it was I who spotted his talents in the first place, but he's finished now. Not just because of the accident, but the way he muffed the jump in the first place. You should have seen the way he took that jump! Useless. I'm beginning to think it's a good thing this has happened. We would have gone on hoping September could win the Western Counties' and he would have let us down. Well he's lame now. And the more I think about it, the

c   65

more I can see the hand of Fate in it.'

Mrs Dewar looked at her husband in total bewilderment. 'What on earth do you mean, Richard? The hand of Fate? You've dreamed for months now of Anna winning the Western Counties'—you've talked about nothing else. Everything's revolved round it even—' there was a tinge of bitterness in her voice—'even Anna going away to school, and having special instruction. Now you talk calmly about Fate.'

'You don't understand.' There was that strange light in Mr Dewar's eyes that Mary had seen before. 'Anna *is* going to win the Western Counties'. Now this has happened we can be certain of it. As long as it's not too late—by George, I hope it isn't—I'm going to buy her King of Prussia.'

'Wha-at?' gasped Mrs Dewar. At the same moment Anna leapt to her feet and came out of September's loose box. She had been kneeling with him all this time, but now, rubbing the back of her sleeve across her tearstained cheek, she too stared at her father in amazement.

'*What* did you say, Daddy?'

'Richard!' Mrs Dewar was placing a hand on her husband's arm. 'You don't know what you're saying. This is becoming madness. We've gambled everything on September, on sending Anna to Kilmingdean, there's nothing left to gamble. There's no possible way we can buy that horse.'

'I can sell the car,' said Mr Dewar shortly. 'And I shall.'

'The car?'

The astonishment felt by Anna and her mother was felt equally by Mary. Mr Dewar's car was several years old, but it was one of the most expensive models in Britain. It was always kept in beautiful condition, polished and gleaming. It was truly his pride and joy.

'That's what I said. We can drive around in the old

66

farm van for a while, until—' he placed an arm round his daughter's shoulders and smiled at her, '—Anna puts everything right for us.'

'Oh, Daddy,' she smiled at him through her tears, 'I know you've sort of got money worries or something, but I *can* put everything right, I know I can, if you buy King. Oh—!' she clapped her hands to her cheeks in excitement tinged with fear. 'I hope we're not too late! Suppose they've already got another buyer for him!'

'Come along, we'll soon find out. We're going to ring the school. Come to my office. You can listen while I put through the call.'

Without so much as a backward glance at September, Anna went out of the stable with her father. Mrs Dewar followed them. As soon as they had gone, Mary rushed and opened the door of September's loose box and knelt down beside him.

He looked so helpless lying there, still in some pain, but quiet and uncomplaining. Everything had happened with such horrible suddenness that Mary's mind had scarcely been able to grasp it. But now the full force of her emotions hit her.

'They've forgotten about you already! They've just left you lying here. Oh, my poor sweet love—'

September whinnied and nudged Mary with his muzzle. At that moment her anguish became unbearable and she leapt to her feet and raced out of the stable into the farm yard. Anna and her father had already disappeared inside the house, but Mrs Dewar was lingering by the dry stone wall outside, pulling up some weeds that were choking the flowers at the foot of the wall.

As Mary raced up to her she straightened up and frowned.

'Oh, hello, Mary. You were still in the stable—?'

'Yes, I'm sorry, I heard but—' The words came out in

a choking sob: 'What's going to become of September? You must tell me, you must.'

'Don't cry, child.'

'What will become of him?' said Mary fiercely.

'He will have to be sold, I'm afraid.' Mrs Dewar broke the news as gently as she could. 'We cannot possible afford to keep two animals. I expect Mr Dewar will try and find a local buyer. Someone who's prepared to nurse him, and take a chance on his getting over his lameness. There must be somebody who would like to buy such a fine horse.'

Mary turned to walk away, but Mrs Dewar called her back.

'In the meantime you must look after him, Mary. I know he couldn't be in better hands. See if he'll take something to eat now. Later on Mr Dewar will show you how to change his poultice. It has to be done three times a day.'

Mary nodded, grateful to have a practical job of work to do.

That evening she pleaded with her father that they should make an offer for September, just as she had begged him so long ago to be allowed to keep the pony that Mr Dewar had wanted to sell. Mr Wilkins had been adamant then, he was even more adamant now.

'Us buy a lame horse and keep him and pay his upkeep? You're wasting your breath girl, asking me, and you know it.'

Later, when he heard Mary crying herself to sleep in bed that night, he came into her little room and awkwardly bent over her bed and touched her on the shoulder.

'I didn't mean to speak like that, girlie. I know how you love that animal. Sometimes I wish I was a rich man, and that's a fact.'

The Dewars succeeded in buying King of Prussia from Kilmingdean School. He would arrive in about one week's time. Mary did not learn this news from Anna, who kept carefully out of her way, but from one of the farm hands. In the meantime, Mr Dewar was trying to find a buyer for September.

Two or three times when Mary was in the stable tending the horse, the farmer arrived with prospective buyers who wished to inspect the animal. Each time her heart would lurch and she would look at their faces, to see if they looked kind, and would give September a good home.

Soon it was common gossip around the farm that Mr Dewar could not find a buyer for September. For two days Mary went around the farm feeling a sense of comfort. If no one wanted to buy September in his present condition, then at least he would have to stay at Chestnut Farm for a few more weeks, and she would have the joyful task of nursing him back to health.

For Mary, reading books on the subject, was becoming more and more convinced that if she could be the one in charge of September's health, she could nurse him back to complete recovery.

On the third day, the day that King of Prussia was due to arrive from Kilmingdean, Mary's father sent her on an errand after breakfast. It was to the village post office, four miles away, and she went by cycle.

On the way back she heard a large vehicle coming up the narrow one-track lane that led from the farm, and she pulled into the hedge and waited for it to pass. It was a tall enclosed van, painted cream with blue lettering on the side. It was only as she cycled on her way that the words written on the van registered on her mind:

Rickards of Silverstock   Licensed Horse Slaughterers

TEN

TO SAVE SEPTEMBER

Mary jammed on her cycle brakes so hard that she almost went over the handlebars. She slewed the bike round in the narrow lane and started pedalling furiously back the way she had come, in pursuit of the van.

It had turned a corner now but she could see its roof peeping above the high hedges of the lane as it bumped slowly along towards the main road. Panting for breath she turned the same corner and saw its back quite clearly as it stopped at the 'T' junction. There were the words again, painted blue on cream, across the double doors at the back: Rickards of Silverstock.

So she had not imagined it!

The vehicle drew out into the main road, turning right, and disappeared from view. It had been to Chestnut Farm to collect something and was now speeding on its way back to Silverstock.

Mary braked when she reached the main road, and rested her head for a moment on the handlebars. Her body was racked with sobs and her eyes were blinded with tears.

'September!' she moaned. 'September!'

To think she had felt complacent for the past two days, ever since she had realized that Mr Dewar could not find a buyer for the lame horse. She had fondly imagined that she would have September for a few weeks longer, would be given the satisfaction of nursing him back to health! The obvious fate for the animal had never even occurred to her. Mr Dewar had sold September to a horse dealer. He was going to be shot.

'No!' she cried aloud. 'I won't let them kill you—I won't —I won't—'

She wiped away the tears with the back of her hand, stood hard on the pedals and shot out into the main road, turning right to Silverstock.

'I haven't a hope of catching up with the van, but I've got to get there just as fast as I can. Before—'

Before it's too late; before they shoot September, whispered her thoughts.

She cycled like the wind, a wild distraught figure, her hair streaming out behind her, through all the little hamlets and villages on the road to Silverstock. White thatched cottages and red brick inns and green fields with cows grazing passed by her in a blur, as her feet pummelled the pedals and her breath came in gasps.

Throughout that nightmare journey she had a vision of September in her mind's eye, the animal she loved more than anything in the world, being led into some terrible dark building with a blanket over his head. He would be alone and friendless and very frightened, he would sense that he had been abandoned. And then a shot would ring out—

Mary's body trembled all over. Supposing it was happening now! Supposing at this very moment the shot was being fired and when she arrived September would be dead. There were some cross-roads ahead, with a sign-post. Silverstock 5 miles it told her, as she flashed by. She had already covered an enormous distance without even noticing it; she would reach the town in a little over half an hour!

As at last her bike turned into the wide main street of the Devonshire market town, she was almost at the end of her strength. Her heart was pounding and her temples were throbbing. Her legs were aching so much that she felt she could pedal no more. She let herself free wheel down the gently sloping street, focusing her attention on a distant policeman.

When she at last drew level with him, she had recovered her breath a little, and tried to sound matter-of-fact as she spoke to him.

'Could you direct me to Rickards, please?'

'You have to turn left down Lower High Street, miss,' he said, looking at her dishevelled appearance with some curiosity. 'Then you take the third turning on the right, Bear Alley, and the slaughterhouse is facing you at the end—'

At the word 'slaughterhouse' Mary's face took on a yellowish tinge and she thought for a moment that she would be sick.

'Is anything wrong, miss? Can I help?'

'N-no nothing, thank you!' she stuttered.

Somehow her feet found the pedals and she hurried on her way.

As the wheels of her bike bumped over the cobbles of Bear Alley she could see the big building at the end. It looked like a warehouse, with big double doors. They were firmly closed. Was September inside there now?

She propped her bike up against a wall and ran over to those doors, pressing her ear against them. At that moment a cloud sailed in front of the sun and the whole sky seemed to turn dark. The building looked gaunt and gloomy now and there was a chilling silence everywhere.

'September?' she whispered. 'Are you in there?'

The only reply was the sound of her own heartbeat, throbbing in her ears.

A narrow tarmac service road ran round the side of the building. She walked along it, in the shadow of the high

building, past a sign that said PRIVATE STRICTLY NO
ADMITTANCE. Then she found herself in a huge yard at the
rear of the building and there, parked in front of her, was
the tall narrow van, its doors firmly closed.

'September!' she cried, racing forward.

She pummelled on the back of the van.

'September!'

For a moment she thought the van was empty, and that
all her worst fears were justified.

Then she heard restless movements inside the van.

'September!'

A long, low whinny came to her ears.

Mary trembled with relief. September was still alive!

'Hey!'

Two men came running out of a hut, where they had
been having some lunch. One of them was still chewing a
sandwich. They were wearing blue overalls with the mono-
gram R on the front.

'What are doing in here?'

'Can't you read?'

'Please don't shoot him!' she blurted out helplessly,
pointing to the closed door. *'Please—'*

'You know the horse then?'

Mary nodded, despairingly.

The older of the two men came and took her firmly by
the arm.

'A young girl like you shouldn't be in here,' he said
gently enough. 'It's not allowed. Come on, where do you
live?'

'Miles away! Chestnut Farm—where you've just come
from! I've cycled all the way, I've never stopped once. As
soon as I realized you'd taken September away. *He can't
die!* He's a beautiful horse, a show-jumper!'

'No love, he's lame now.'

'But his leg will get better, I know it will!'

73

'Get her out of here, Mike. It's for the best.'

'No!' Mary started to struggle. 'I'm not leaving!'

A man came out from a nearby building. He was wearing tweeds.

'What on earth's going on here?'

'It's this girl, Mr. Rickard. She's upset because Mr Dewar's horse has got to be destroyed.'

'Now look here, young lady,' said the boss, 'this horse is our property, it's paid for, and what we do with it is none of your business. I must also remind you that you are on private property and ask you to leave the premises at once.'

At any other time Mary would have been frightened of such a stern forbidding man. There was a hard look about his eyes that she did not like at all. But she knew that September's life was at stake, and that she must fight for it. Up to now she had not even paused to think *how* she could rescue September, only that he must be saved.

As her mind raced desperately over the possibilties she remembered something that lay in the saddlebag on her cycle. It was her Post Office Savings Book. She had regularly put away the money that Mr Dewar had been paying her for working as a groom. This morning, as usual, she had paid two pounds into her account while buying her father's postal order at the village post office.

'Supposing I offered to buy him from you?' she said quickly.

'What?' Mr. Rickard looked at her and smiled in amusement. 'A youngster like you? You haven't got that sort of money.'

'I've got a lot of money in my Post Office Savings!' said Mary. She *had* to make him take her seriously. 'And I've got my book with me! If you don't believe me, I'll go and get it.'

'Very well.'

Mary turned and ran back along the service road, right round the side of the big building, to the wall at the front where she had parked her bike. With trembling fingers she unfastened her saddlebag and pulled out the precious blue book: *National Savings Bank*—proclaimed the cover, *Ordinary Account.*

Without even pausing to do up the straps again she turned and raced back down the side of the building. Her head was down as she ran; out of the corner of her eye she glimpsed that forbidding sign *Strictly No Admittance* ahead of her, but she did not even see the gate. She crashed straight into it.

She had been unaware of the gate before as the men had left it wide open when driving the van through, and had not bothered to close it. But it was closed now, a tall wire mesh gate, firmly padlocked, completely sealing off the narrow road. She had been tricked!

'Let me through!' she cried.

She could see the van in the yard. Its doors were open now and the men in blue overalls were leading September down the ramp, under the watchful eye of their boss. September was moving his head from side to side, restless and frightened, and the men were having difficulty with him.

The sight of the beloved horse was too much for Mary.

'Let me through!' she screamed. She waved the blue book. 'I *have* got a lot of money.' Mary had accumulated nearly forty pounds from present money since early childhood, as well as saving all her earnings for the past three months. By her standards her life savings constituted a small fortune. '*I've* got sixty-four pounds!'

'And I paid eighty for this animal!' shouted Mr. Rickard. 'Now go away child, just go away!'

Mary clung to the wire gate, and started to sob. They

were leading September across the yard now, towards the back of the big grim building.

She did not even hear the old motor bike coming up behind her, until it braked by her side. Her father was sitting astride it, his face like a thundercloud.

'Dad!' she gasped.

'I've been looking for you everywhere. I might have guessed you'd come here.'

'They're going to kill September!' she cried.

'I know, girl, I know.'

Then John Wilkins did a strange thing. He put a hand on the horn of his motor bike and kept it there. He was usually such a quiet man, but now he was making the most deafening row that Mary had ever heard.

ELEVEN

A WONDERFUL SECRET

'Dad!' gasped Mary, putting her hands over her ears. 'What—what are you doing?'

As he pressed the horn of his motor-bike relentlessly, the whole world seemed filled with noise. *Bir—bir—bir—BIR—BIRRR!* With the high wall of the slaughterhouse on one side of them, and a tall fence on the other, they were in a kind of tunnel which made the noise reverberate further.

John Wilkins knew exactly what he was doing.

The two men had led September down the ramp of the horse box and were now trying to get him across to the main building. He had been restless before, but now he was almost uncontrollable as the motor-bike horn blasted forth on the other side of the locked gate.

'Calm down, old fellow—*calm down!*'

September would not calm down. He had looked towards the gate and recognized Mary. He knew that the motor-bike horn was blaring out some desperate message.

Bir—bir—BIRRRRRRR!

He reared up on his hind legs and kicked out at the two men; it took all their strength to hang on to him and save him from bolting.

For the past two minutes Mr Rickard had tried to ignore the presence of Mary and her father, but now he could ignore it no longer.

77

He hurried over to the high gate and peered through it.

'Stop that noise!' he shouted over the din. 'What d'you think you're trying to do.'

John Wilkins took his hand off the horn. Now all was silent.

'Unlock that gate and let us in,' he said quietly.

'Why—why should I? This is private property.'

'Because I'm going to buy that animal,' said John Wilkins.

He felt in the back pocket of his trousers and pulled out a thick roll of bank notes. Mary stared at the bank notes and then at her father in disbelief. She looked at the blue bank book in her hands.

'Dad—I've got sixty-four pounds, we only need another sixteen.'

'Put that away,' said her father shortly. He climbed off his motor-bike, propped it up, and walked right up to the gate. He grabbed the wire mesh and rattled it 'Come on, open up. You paid eighty, did you? Well, I'll give you eighty-five.'

Mr Rickard eyed the thick roll of notes with approval, and then glanced across at September, who was still giving his men a great deal of trouble.

'Done,' he said.

The big gate was unlocked and Mary and her father walked through. While he went into one of the buildings with Mr Rickard to sign the necessary papers, she clung to September, feeling weak in the legs from her long cycle ride, and almost faint with relief and joy.

'You're safe,' she whispered, over and over again.

He was quite calm now, and nuzzled her cheek, as if to say 'thank you'.

Mary felt September's warm body against her side and heard his heart beating strongly. A bird on a nearby tree burst into song. It was the sweetest moment of her life.

After they had bought September, father and daughter walked him very slowly out of the town to Uncle Henry's. John Wilkins' brother Henry owned his own small farm on the outskirts of Silverstock, and would be able to borrow a horse-box.

'Can't Mary ride him to Chestnut Farm?' asked Henry, not noticing that the horse was lame.

They quickly pointed this out to him.

'Besides, he's got to arrive under cover of darkness, Henry. I don't want the boss to know I've bought him. Bring him over to the cottage tonight, the later the better.'

'If you say so, John,' said Henry. He did not question his brother; both the Wilkins were men of a few words. Instead he turned to Mary. 'Put him out in the orchard to graze, there's a good girl.'

Before leaving September in the orchard, Mary hugged him warmly.

'It's goodbye, but just for a few hours. I'm going to clean out our big shed when I get home and put down plenty of warm straw, all ready for you to sleep on tonight.'

When she got back to the house, her father was preparing to leave.

'Good of you to lend me the money, Henry,' he was saying gruffly. 'You'll get it back in a few weeks' time, every penny.'

'Of course I will, John.'

They walked back through the town together to collect their respective vehicles. Mary glanced up at her father's weatherbeaten face and felt very tender towards him. He was a poor man and she had wondered how he had managed to find so much money all at once. Now she knew.

Of course, there was no question of their keeping September for good; Mary had realized that from the beginning.

'You'll pay Uncle Henry back when—when we sell September?' she asked timidly.

'Aye, that's the idea.'

'And you think we *will* be able to sell him?' she said, very bright eyed. 'That there's no need at all for him to be destroyed.'

'I've talked to men who know horses,' he said. 'And I've been reading them books you've got out of the library. It needs time and patience, and a bit o' love, to get that animal right as rain. And my little girl's got all three.'

'Oh, Dad!' Mary grabbed hold of his big hand as they walked along, her heart almost bursting with happiness. She had never heard him make such a speech. 'I *know* I can get him better. And then lots of people will want to buy him; we can pick and choose and find him the nicest home. . . .'

Her voice faltered and secretly she thought: *The nicest home we can and somewhere nearby, so I can still go on seeing him.* She did not want to think about being parted from September, yet. She would not think about it!

'Wait here, Mary,' said her father, stopping by a hardware shop.

When he came out he was carrying some bottles in a bag.

'We'll have to get busy tonight and dye his coat.'

'September's?' said Mary in surprise.

'Aye. We'll keep him in the shed and graze him on our garden, and there's no reason for the Dewars to see him— but we can't take any chances.'

'Do you think Mr Dewar would be angry if he found out?'

'Very angry. We've interfered in his private affairs, you see. And he doesn't see reason about that horse. He thinks he's seen the back of him for good.'

'If he hates September now it's unfair!' said Mary angrily. '*He* made him lame. It was *his* fault. Even Mrs Dewar thinks so.'

'Aye. And nobody likes to be reminded of their mistakes.

If he finds out what I've done, it could cost me my job.'

Those words shocked Mary into silence.

On the long cycle ride back to Chestnut Farm she had plenty of time to think about the risk that her father had taken, for her sake and September's, and how very careful she would have to be in the coming weeks.

He had got home before her, of course, and was already busy about the farm, working hard to make up for the time spent in Silverstock.

He ate the huge meal that Mary cooked him and then went straight out to work again. As Mary washed up their plates, her thoughts turned to Anna for the first time that day. How had *she* taken the loss of September? To think they had once been such dear friends, so close, sharing every experience, big and small. Now something of absolute enormity had happened on the farm, and she had no idea what Anna was thinking or feeling.

There was something terrible about a friendship grown distant.

'Yet I still think Anna's the same person underneath. The way she sobbed about September's leg last week, that was the *real Anna*. It's that horrible, snobby school that's made her seem different,' mused Mary. She was returning, as always, to her innermost secret hope: that Anna had fallen under some kind of spell which she must surely awaken from as time went on.

'How can she prefer King of Prussia to September?' thought Mary, angrily. 'And how can she like a stuck-up girl like Delphine when *we've* been best friends for years and years.'

Mary had to fight down the jealousy that welled up inside her and made her feel almost ill. Why had Anna been avoiding her ever since she got home for the holidays? She had to see her, speak to her again, if only to know how she was feeling about September.

81

It was then that Mary heard Anna's footsteps coming up the lane.

The two girls met at the garden gate of Primrose Cottage, face to face. Mary tried to appear calm, but her heart seemed to lurch inside her. She had so much to make her happy today, and she could not help but feel happy now. Here was Anna, her playmate from childhood, her hair as blonde as Mary's was dark. They were both grown tall and slender now, still just about the same height. Foolishly she remembered how, as little girls, they were always measuring each other against the barn wall, seeing who could grow the faster.

'Hello, Mary.'

For the first time since she had got home from Kilmingdean, Anna had come to seek her out.

'Hello, Anna.'

'It—it's simply awful about September, isn't it?'

Mary blushed. Looking into Anna's eyes, she realized that she had been crying a lot. So she cared about losing September, she really did care!

Hope was coursing through Mary's veins again. This was the old Anna! She felt close to her again, just for those few moments, and she longed to cry out her wonderful secret : *He isn't dead, Anna! He's alive! He's coming back to Chestnut Farm and I'm going to make him better.*

Instead she nodded silently and looked down at her hands, unable to meet Anna's eye. It was terrible to have to allow her to think that September had been destroyed.

When she looked up the bright artificial smile that Anna seemed to have acquired at Kilmingdean was now in evidence.

'I wondered if you'd like to come and meet King of Prussia?'

'Your new horse?' asked Mary. Why did she feel so shocked? 'Has—has he arrived then, already?'

82

'Yes, he came this morning. He's in the stable. Come on!'

Anna had grabbed Mary's arm and was pulling her through the gate. Mary allowed herself to be pulled along down the lane and into the farmyard, but her feet were dragging; her whole body stiff and rebellious.

'Come on! What's the matter?'

Anna was too excited to notice or care that Mary did not want to come into the stable. She gave her a good-humoured shove so that Mary tottered in through the doorway.

'There he is. Did you ever see such a beauty?'

As Mary stared at the animal in the loose box, anger welled up inside her. This was *September's* stable. This much vaunted horse, King of Prussia, must have arrived almost immediately after September's departure. He must have taken up residence in the loose box while the straw was still warm from September's beloved presence.

While she had known all along that King of Prussia was due to arrive some time today, it was only the sight of his physical presence that really brought it home to Mary. The heartlessness of Mr Dewar: the cruelty of it! All so he could win his stupid old championship!

Surely Anna could see how horrible it was?

But no. Mary watched in angry silence as the other girl walked into the loose box and threw her arms round the horse's neck.

'You've come home, King. You're mine now, really mine.'

Mary came out of the stable; Anna followed her.

'Don't you like him?'

'He's all right,' Mary shrugged.

He was a beautiful horse, true enough; a thoroughbred, and perfectly in proportion. He was a small, neat animal in contrast to the rather gawky-looking September. He had a fine dark brown gleaming coat which was altogether more elegant than September's mixture of russet and brown like autumn leaves. He also had, Mary decided, a very haughty expression. Perhaps he had picked it up at Kilmingdean.

'What are you doing, Anna?' came a stern voice.

Mr Dewar had suddenly appeared. Although he was speaking to Anna he was glaring at Mary.

'Just—just showing King to Mary, Daddy.'

'Why? Haven't you explained to her that her services as a groom won't be required now that you are home?'

'It's not fair, Daddy!' Anna suddenly said petulantly. 'None of the other girls at school have to muck out stables and things like that.'

'Perhaps their fathers have more money than I have,' said Mr Dewar bad-temperedly. 'As you are perfectly well aware, Anna.'

To see Anna a stranger again, talking about her as a paid servant made something snap inside Mary. She spoke with a forthrightness that left her surprised at herself.

'It's just as well you don't want me as a groom. I've got plenty of other things to do these holidays. And besides— I don't like the look of your new horse all that much. He's not a patch on September.'

With that she turned on her heel and walked away, conscious of the fact that Anna and her father were staring after her in astonishment.

As Mary opened the back gate and went into the big garden of Primrose Cottage, a tear trickled down her cheek. The few moments of closeness with Anna were almost too much to bear thinking about. The flame of friendship had flickered into life, only to be immediately extinguished.

'It's almost as though there's too much between Anna and I now. Not just the school, not just King of Prussia, but Mr Dewar as well. He doesn't think I'm good enough for

84

her, and that's a big influence on her. Will things *ever* be the same again?'

She felt all alone, and near to despair.

Yet as she set to work to clear out the big wooden shed that was to be September's home, her spirits began to revive. She began to day-dream about what fantastic things she might do this summer.

TWELVE

FACE TO FACE

The next few weeks were, in one way, the happiest that Mary had ever known.

September was hers—her very own! Of course it was only an interlude. He would have to be sold so that her father could pay Uncle Henry back, there was no doubt about that. But for the moment he was *hers,* living here at Primrose Cottage: to love and cherish and to nurse. She would get his lame leg completely better, she was determined about that.

At night she could see him from her bedroom window, sleeping out on the piece of rough ground at the far end of their garden : just glimpse him between the trees. It was turning into a beautiful summer, most nights warm and balmy and dry, so that the times when she had to bring September into their big shed and settle him down on straw for the night because of the rain or cold were few.

It was so lovely to see him out there, settling down to sleep, last thing at night before she herself climbed into bed and put out the light.

Of course, he looked completely different these days. His coat was no longer russet and dappled brown, but a dull black colour. Mary's father had seen to that with the mysterious and most effective bottles that he had bought from the shop in Silverstock. It had given Mary a shock at first to see September so utterly changed in appearance and she knew that the colour did not suit him. He looked gawky at the best of times and now without his shining coat he looked a very ordinary horse indeed.

However, she had soon got used to the change, and all that mattered was that he was the same beloved horse underneath, and that their secret was safe. Primrose Cottage was tucked away and although people like the postman came and called, there was no reason for anyone to go exploring round the back where September grazed each day on the Wilkins' piece of ground, which was cut off from sight of the rest of the farm by high hedges and trees. Nevertheless, if anyone did by chance catch a glimpse of him, he was just a horse—any old horse—who certainly looked nothing like September, and not an eyebrow would be raised.

'Henry saw him this afternoon,' John Wilkins told his daughter at supper one day, referring to one of the farm hands. 'He brought some scraps round for the chickens while we were out, and took them round the back. He's just asked me about him.'

'What did you say, Dad?' asked Mary, slightly alarmed.

'I said he was my brother's nag and I was taking care o' him for a while,' said John Wilkins.

'Did he notice the bandage, do you think?'

'I think not,' her father frowned. 'Or if he did, he thought nothing on it. Seems September's passed his first test.'

Mary nodded and glanced at her father with concern. She knew that he hated deception of any kind and that all this was a great strain to him. It would be a great relief when the bandage could come off, for that was the one thing that might lead people to connect the horse with September.

From the beginning Mary had known that the one great danger was Anna. For all their past summers Anna had been

87

in and out of Primrose Cottage as though it were her own home, and had treated the Wilkins' garden as her own. Many times they had lingered there, talking, picking flowers, and sometimes just lying in the long grass and whispering all their secrets to each other.

If Anna should wander in the garden just once, looking for Mary, and should chance upon September while his leg was still strapped up—then she, indeed, might recognize him.

However, as the days passed and Anna never came by, Mary knew that her secret was safe. It should have filled her with great relief and happiness, instead it filled her with an aching sense of loneliness.

Anna had not forgiven her for not liking King of Prussia, for making it clear how much she preferred September. She would have nothing to do with Mary now. The two friends were completely estranged and for the first time in the whole of her life Mary was spending the long summer holidays with no one to talk to, no one to share things with.

So although these few weeks were, in one way, the happiest that Mary had ever known, in another way they were not.

Just as Anna carefully avoided Mary, she too took great care to keep out of Anna's way. She knew that she was with King of Prussia a great deal of the time, grooming him and exercising him, and continually taking him round the practice course that they had erected on the water meadow, taking the jumps under the anxious and watchful eye of her father.

Secretly, Mary would have loved to have watched her— to have compared the new horse's performance with September's before he became lame, to try and assess Anna's chances of winning the Western Counties' Championship.

Instead, she stayed well clear, concentrating all her attention on September's well being.

For the first few days she poulticed his leg every three hours, as the books told her to, and forced him to lie down on the straw in the stuffy shed for as long as possible each day.

'I know you hate it in here,' she would say, stroking his mane to calm down his restless spirit, 'and that you'd much rather be out in the sunshine. But there's too much to distract you out there and I *know* you won't lie down once you're outside.'

September, who now felt quite well in himself and was no longer feeling any pain from the leg, did not really understand. But Mary knew how important these first two weeks were. September must not take any more weight on the leg than absolutely necessary until all traces of swelling had gone, on that fact depended his chances of complete recovery.

He did not understand, but he could not bear Mary to be displeased, so after the first few tussles he gave in to her with good grace. One day when she came into the shed unexpectedly she caught him standing up in the home-made loose box that her father had built, trying to nibble some plants hanging on the wall of the shed.

Guiltily he sunk down on to his knees on his bed of straw, hiding his face from her and pretending that he had been in that position all the time.

'You naughty boy!' Mary could not help laughing. 'But at least I can tell you've got the message at last.'

Thanks to her caution, the swelling had completely disappeared in ten days, and she could begin to give him gentle exercise, walking him slowly round the garden and letting him stay out to graze.

It was another three weeks before the supporting bandages could come off, and only then could Mary and her father breathe freely.

'Now nobody will guess who you are,' she said, giving

him a triumphant hug. 'Not even Anna herself.'

Anna! The very name made Mary ache a little. How was she getting on with King of Prussia? Was he still the most wonderful horse in the world to her? Mary's curiosity was growing all the time as the day of the Western Counties' Championship drew nearer, but she was determined to control it. Besides, she still had a lot to do. Now September was entering the most important period of his convalescence.

The bandage was off and he was walking well, and all sign of damage to the leg had gone. But he was walking with a limp, as though there were a weakness there. Was it going to be a permanent weakness, or could it be cured?

'There's only one hope of getting you perfect again, September,' she told him. 'And we're going to start today. Come on, we're going for a swim in the sea.'

There was an ideal place. Not the big cove where she and Anna had gone to so often in the old days to gallop him across the sands. That would be too dangerous for it meant going right through the farm with September, and besides, Anna often exercised King of Prussia on the wide expanse of beach. They must not meet up, whatever happened!

Instead she took him by way of a narrow track that was hardly ever used. It encircled the farm to the North and was buried between high hedgerows for most of the way, almost like a secret tunnel. It led direct to a cleft in the low-lying cliffs, round the headland from where the wide beaches were, to a steep path that led straight down into a deep rock pool. In the old days she and Anna had sometimes swum there together and called it their secret oasis, for nobody ever went there.

The first day Mary led September gently down the steep path and then, taking off her shoes and socks so that she wore only shorts and shirt, plunged into the water first.

'Come on, boy, in you come,' she cajoled. 'It's beautiful!'

After some hesitation, the horse plunged in beside her and was soon swimming strongly in the big pool and enjoying every moment of it.

Mary knew from the books that this was the best possible therapy for the weak leg, exercising it and bringing strength back to the muscles, without imposing any weight or strain upon them. They made the secret expedition every day, and each day she let September swim a little longer than the day before.

It was, of course, expensive on dye. The harsh salt water played havoc with September's black coat, and there was always plenty of touching up to do as soon as they got back to Primrose Cottage. Mary's father grumbled at the expense but he was as thrilled as she was to see that the treatment was working and the leg improving, day by day.

Just one week before the Western Counties' Championship was due to take place the cure was complete. September's limp had finally disapeared, all trace of it, and he was once again perfect in every way.

'It's a miracle, girl,' said her father. 'He's a fine horse again, still a great show-jumper I daresay. We'll find him a good home now—we'll pick and choose and find just the right buyer for him.'

'Yes, Dad.' Mary could not bear to think of them selling September. She *would* not think of it—not yet! 'If it's all right with you, I'm going to take him for a swim. One last swim. We enjoy them so much.'

The sun was hot that morning and they stayed in the water longer than ever before. September was better, completely fit again! That thought filled Mary with happiness, but it was a bitter-sweet happiness. *Must* it come to an end?

As she let the gentle waves lap round them, one arm round September's neck, Mary let herself day-dream again. Not for the first time she was indulging in a secret fantasy that refused to go away.

When they finally came out of the water, September's coat looked much worse than usual. In some places the black was now just a shabby grey and in other places his russet coat actually showed through, making him look like a scruffy piebald.

They cantered back along the narrow track, brushing the hedgerow in places. Mary could feel the hot sun drying her shorts and shirt to her skin. For a moment she fancied that the sound of September's hooves were echoing along the lane and then, as they turned a sharp bent, she knew that it was not an echo, but the hoofbeats of another horse.

Anna was coming this way, mounted upon King of Prussia, and in a moment they would be face to face.

THIRTEEN

THE PLAN

Mary reined in September and brought him to a standstill as Anna came up on King of Prussia. They were trapped together in the narrow lane. Anna brought her horse to a halt just a few feet away from them and silently the two girls faced each other.

King of Prussia was beautifully groomed and looking very elegant, the same haughty expression on his face that Mary had noticed before. He seemed to be surveying September with supercilious distaste.

It was not the horse's expression that caught Mary's attention though, it was Anna's. For a few brief, unguarded moments Anna did not think to compose herself and Mary saw clearly a lost, sad look in her eyes.

So although she should have felt shock and alarm at meeting Anna like this, and fear that she would recognize September, quite a different emotion rushed through Mary.

Anna was unhappy! It was unmistakable.

What was she doing on this lonely, hidden track? It led nowhere but to the secret cleft in the cliffs and the path and the deep rock pool. It was *their* place, Mary's and Anna's, their 'secret oasis' where they used to come and swim in summers past, summers happier than this one.

Had Anna come down here to remember happier times? Was she missing Mary's friendship after all, feeling as lonely as Mary was herself?

Then suddenly, Anna read Mary's thoughts and went pink with embarrassment. Now Mary was positive that she had guessed correctly. She longed to cry out: 'Oh, Anna, isn't this silly! Can't we be friends again—*can't we*?' Instead she stared down at the ground.

When she looked up again Anna's face was cold and expressionless. She was furious at having been caught out heading for the place that was a symbol of her lost friendship with Mary—furious that Mary should have seen her blush.

'So it's true,' she drawled, 'you have got a horse this summer? Looking after it for your uncle or something, aren't you?'

'That's right,' mumbled Mary, at the same time moving forward close against the hedgerow, trying to get past Anna. September was in such a mess after his swim in the sea, some of the black dye had come clean off his coat and the russet showed through. She mustn't let Anna recognize him, she mustn't! 'Been for a swim. Got to get back now and cook Dad's lunch, I'm late. . . .'

Typically Anna made no move but sat there squarely on King of Prussia, almost completely blocking the track and forcing September right into the bank.

In a panic to get past quickly, Mary spurred September on to a trot and the horse slithered on the grassy bank and almost tripped over a trailing root before they were safely past. Mary and the horse quickly recovered their balance but not before they had both looked undignified and clumsy—and Anna's laughter was ringing out, laughter that was brittle and false.

'What a nag!' she sneered. 'What a rag bag! I know you don't like King and I'm not in the least bit offended that you never show any interest in how we're getting on, but to think you've been spending all your time with *that* broken-down animal. Really!'

As Mary galloped on along the track, Anna's mocking words rang in her brain and made the blood pound in her temples. Suddenly she was angry, angrier than she had ever been in her life.

'So that's what she thinks, is it?' she said between clenched teeth. 'Did you hear what she said about you, September? Did you?'

When she got near the farm, she took September off the track, up the bank and through a gap in the hedge, and out into an open field. At the far end of the field was a five-barred gate.

'Come on, boy! Let's go!'

They started at a canter and then gradually built up speed, flying across the wide expanse of meadow, September's hooves hardly seeming to touch the green turf beneath. It was the most wonderful experience to be doing this with September again! Mary's dark hair was streaming out behind her in the breeze and her whole body throbbed with exhilaration as she felt the horse, so sure and confident with every stride, between the inside of her knees. They were heading straight for the gate!

'Over!'

He soared over with skill and grace and together they made a perfect landing. In that moment Mary's last doubts were removed. September was fitter than he had ever been, still the great show-jumper. She realized something else. The horse she loved so much could jump for her better than for anyone else in the world!

She slowed him down to a walk, his chest heaving, letting him recover from his exertion. Mary, too, was breathing very fast, but not because of the exertion. The thing she had day-dreamed about for weeks, but never dared to think of putting into practice, was now taking on an air of reality.

'If we could do it,' she whispered to September. 'It could change everything.'

But first there was one thing she had to know for certain. She had heard rumours around the farm, but now she must try and see with her own eyes whether they were true or not.

For six long weeks, ever since King of Prussia had arrived at the farm, she had deliberately kept away from the water meadow, refusing to see how he and Anna performed together, but she could keep away no longer.

The time had come when she must see September's rival in action. Suddenly it was a matter of extreme urgency!

In fact, Mary had to contain her impatience until the middle of the following afternoon.

After lunch she saw several cars arriving at the old thatched farmhouse and she sensed at once that something important was going to happen. It seemed that Mr Dewar had invited several friends over to see Anna and the horse in action, for the Western Counties' Championship was now only six days away.

When they all went out to the water meadow shortly after three o'clock, there was an unseen onlooker. Mary had taken up residence in a clump of thick bushes on the far side of the meadow. It was a perfect vantage point. She could see everything that went on without being seen herself.

Whatever happened she was not going to give Anna the satisfaction of thinking she was 'taking an interest' at last.

There was an air of expectancy as Anna mounted King of Prussia and cantered him round the meadow to loosen up. Mary had to admit to herself that they made a most distinguished sight. Anna was wearing new jodhpurs and riding boots and a beautiful tailored white shirt with a crisply starched collar. Her long fair hair had been well brushed and was matched in its shining perfection only by the horse's gleaming dark brown coat. For the first time, viewing him from this distance, Mary could see how beautifully proportioned the horse was, everything about him was neat and compact from the top of his glorious mane to the tip of his freshly docked tail.

'All right, Anna,' called out Mr Dewar. 'Start when I ring the bell—and remember you're riding against the clock.'

He was holding a large stop-watch in his hand; he made an adjustment to it and then he shook a small hand-bell that he had taken from his pocket. It rang out clearly across the meadow and Anna started to ride towards the first jump, a fiercely determined expression on her face.

Mary watched closely as they took jump after jump. King of Prussia took each jump neatly enough, but Mary found herself holding her breath each time, not sure whether the small animal would make it or not. It seemed that Anna was having to work very hard to get him over safely each time and when they got to the 'Demon's Dyke', Mary could hardly bear to look.

Yet King of Prussia cleared this jump safely, too, seeming to defy all the laws of gravity as his body wreathed itself over the top and his rear hooves kicked up free of the high brushwood wall at the last possible moment.

'He's efficient, all right,' reflected Mary, 'like a little robot. He's been schooled and schooled . . . but he's not a patch on September, who's just naturally brilliant and faster, I'm sure, *much* faster . . .'

It was over the matter of King of Prussia's speed, or lack of it, that Mary had heard rumours recently. It seemed that Mr Dewar had been getting angry at the slow times he had been doing round the course and, the angrier he got, the slower the little horse seemed to go. In the next few moments Mary saw those stories confirmed at first hand.

There was a dutiful burst of applause as Anna finished the course and Mr Donaldson, one of the group of family friends, called out:

'A clear round, Anna. Well done!'

But Mr Dewar was striding over to his daughter, the stop-watch in his hand, and his face like thunder. A slight shiver ran through Mary for she had seen that expression so often before, when September had behaved erratically, earlier in the summer.

'He's slower than ever today, Anna! This isn't going to win us the Western Counties', y'know!'

'He jumped beautifully!' said Anna defensively. She dismounted from the horse and stroked his neck protectively, as though daring her father to say another word against him. 'No one's ever complained that he's slow before. Just look at all the trophies he's won!'

'Local events, most of them,' snapped Mr Dewar. 'This is a national event at Imchester next week—you'll be up against some of the best riders in the country.'

'Well, you must admit he's better than September,' said Anna, anxious to deflect her father's annoyance.

'Of course he is. He's reliable. It's just his speed, we've got to get it up, my girl.'

For a few moments Mary had felt some sympathy for Anna, but now her anger was reawakened. She could not wait to get away from the meadow, unseen, and return to the cottage. She had a lot to tell September!

'They think you were unreliable, my love,' she said. 'How *can* they talk about you like that when as far as they're concerned you—you're dead.' She closed her eyes for a moment, reliving all the terrible emotions of that day six weeks ago. Then she opened them again, put a hand on September's neck, and took a breath: she had some absolutely momentous news to break to him!

'We're going to bring Anna back to her senses, you and

I. She needs a shock, and that's just what we're going to give her.'

Pictures flashed through Mary's mind: Anna on the track yesterday, laughing in that brittle way, calling September a 'rag-bag'. Anna speaking petulantly to her father, referring to Mary as one might to a servant: 'It's not fair, Daddy! None of the other girls at school have to muck out stables and things like that.'

Then another memory came of the day on the beach when Anna had fastened her St Christopher chain round Mary's neck: 'I won't be any different, just because I'm going away to school. I promise. You'll always be my best friend, Mary, nothing will ever change that.'

The time had come to break the spell that held Anna in its thrall, to show her that the things she had come to despise were not to be despised at all.

'*We're* going to win the Western Counties' Championship, September,' said Mary, in a calm voice. 'You and I together.'

FOURTEEN

TO IMCHESTER

Once Mary had made up her mind, she was surprised at how simple everything seemed. Each step in her plan followed logically. Each obstacle that had to be overcome she dealt with in a matter of fact way. She was absolutely single-minded in her determination to take September to Imchester.

Leaving the horse grazing on the piece of rough ground beyond her father's fruit bushes, she cycled the four miles to the red telephone kiosk outside the village post office and, with plenty of change in her pocket, shut herself in the private little world that it afforded. She thumbed through the bright yellow directory until she found the number she wanted.

'I want to enter the Western Counties' Championship please,' she said to the official at the Imchester Course who answered the 'phone. She was speaking in her most grown-up voice. 'Do you still have entry forms?'

'Name and address, please.'

Mary gave them and then asked:

'Can you tell me what the entrance fee is, please?'

'Ten pounds, madam. Send it back with the entry form: I'll see you get one in the morning. Cutting it a bit fine, aren't you? Entries close on Thursday.'

'Thursday?' said Mary, startled. Then, in a firm voice: 'You'll have my form by then, definitely.'

'Could you tell me the name of the horse? I'll make a note of it.'

Mary had thought this out in advance. She could not possibly enter September under his real name! Anna and her family must have no advance warning of what she was doing. Even during the championship itself they need have no inkling that the horse she was riding was September, whom, of course, they believed to be dead some six weeks. She would break the news to Anna afterwards: after they had excelled themselves, done better in the championship than Anna on King of Prussia, after—if Mary had her way —they had won it!

Mary knew now that there was some kind of chemistry that worked between her and September. Together he became more than just a fine show-jumper but perhaps a champion of champions. Even so, to win the Western Counties', against some of the best-known jumpers in Britain would require all this—and good fortune as well.

'His name is Good Fortune,' she said, quite calmly.

'Right—Mary Wilkins on Good Fortune. I've got a note of it, but mind you get the form in.'

With those words the pips sounded and their conversation ended.

Mary walked out of the 'phone box and into the village post office, took her blue Savings Bank book out of her pocket and asked if she might withdraw ten pounds. She filled in the necessary form with a flourish, as though it were something she did every day, and walked out with two crisp five pounds notes. She had never held so much money in her hand all at once, yet now it seemed the most natural thing in the world to be not merely holding it but to be planning to part with it.

Gambling it away, on a ridiculous dream, Dad would think, thought Mary, but the thought did not deject her.

Now she had another telephone call to make, and this

was perhaps the most important part of all. It was to her Uncle Henry.

They spoke on the 'phone for a long time, with Mary doing most of the talking, and when she put the receiver down there was a smile on her lips. Everything was going so smoothly! Who would have dreamt that Uncle Henry would be such a sport and see things just as she did? Fate must surely be on her side.

When she had cycled back to Primrose Cottage and wheeled her bike in through the back gate she saw that her father was with September. It was not often that he had time to spare to take an interest in the horse but at the moment he was walking him across the grass and gazing at his foreleg action with close interest.

The sight of them gave Mary a small shock and she hurried over.

'Anything wrong Dad?'

'Wrong? Of course not, girlie. I've been meaning to look at him for a couple o' days, just to see if there's any sign of the limp coming back. But he's A1, he really is.'

'Of course he is, Dad—' began Mary, a worried feeling in the pit of her stomach. She knew that her father was as honest and straightforward as any man could be and that he had entered into this conspiracy with Mary for her sake, and hers alone. He disliked having the horse that Mr Dewar had despatched to the slaughterhouse and never wanted to see again, here in his garden in secret, his coat disguised with black dye. He did not want the conspiracy to go on a day longer than was necessary.

'You've done a good job, Mary,' he said, as gently as he could, 'but the time's come to sell him now. There's a lot of money I've got to pay Henry back for a start, as well as the expense of keeping him—yes, and the worry, too. I thought I'd put an ad. in Friday's paper—'

'Dad—' began Mary.

'It's all right,' he said, seeing her look of alarm. 'We'll pick him the best home we can. Someone local, someone who'll let you ride him sometimes. I could get a lot of money for him now he's fit again, but I'll let him go really cheap, just to cover my costs, and make it a condition that you see him sometimes.'

'Oh, Dad!' Her father's thoughtfulness brought a lump to Mary's throat, but she had to stop him acting so quickly! 'That wasn't what I was upset about. You see, it's Uncle Henry, I've promised him—'

'Henry?'

'Yes, I've just been and 'phoned him. I've told him about September and he can hardly believe it. He's tickled pink. He wants to see him with his own eyes before we sell him. In fact,' Mary drew a deep breath and glanced at her father anxiously, 'he's asked me to bring him over there on Sunday night and stay the night and enter September for something on Monday and see if we can win.'

'Some little local show, eh?'

Mary blushed. So far she had told her father the literal truth, but the Western Counties' Championship could by no stretch of the imagination be described thus, so she did not reply. Luckily her father did not question her further. He was not a talkative man.

'Well that settles it then. I'll not put the ad. in till next week.'

'Thanks, Dad!' Mary took his hand. 'Then I can go?'

'Of course.'

She went in the house to cook their tea. The last obstacle was removed! She hated deceiving her father, she had never done such a thing before, but she knew that never in a thousand years would he agree to her competing against the boss's daughter at Imchester. It *had* to be kept a secret from him.

'He doesn't understand human nature,' Uncle Henry, a

more worldly man than his brother, had remarked to Mary on the 'phone. 'If you do badly at Imchester you can just pretend you're riding your Uncle's old nag, and the Dewars will feel smug and superior. If you do well, then maybe they'll see you and the horse with new eyes, eh? And, of course, if you walk off with the jackpot, well just think of it!'

Oddly enough the matter of the prize money had not occupied Mary's thoughts at all, even though it represented a fortune that was surely beyond her father's dreams. But for the Dewars to see them with new eyes—yes! Uncle Henry had pin-pointed exactly the reason that was compelling Mary along the unforeseen and dramatic path that she was treading. She would make the scales drop from Anna's eyes at Imchester. If it was humanly possible, she would do it!

Luckily John Wilkins was out milking when the postman arrived the following morning. With cool efficiency Mary asked him to sit down while she ripped open the envelope from Imchester. She filled in the entry form, folded it round the two five pound notes and then sealed it in a fresh envelope already stamped and addressed.

'Will you make *certain* it catches the post?' she pleaded.

'I'll put it in the bag myself when I get back,' smiled the postman, and then went whistling on his way.

The deed was done.

'And now we have four precious nights before we go to Uncle Henry's,' Mary explained to September when she gave him his morning feed. 'I'm afraid we're going to be up some very strange hours. We're going to work by moonlight, you and I, and you'll just have to lie in, in the mornings to make up for it!'

Mary intended that September should become utterly confident about the Demon's Dyke, the Chestnut Farm version of it, by Monday.

'Remember how you did it for me once before?' whispered Mary as they rode out to the meadow that first night, long after everyone had gone to bed. 'It was a clear night, just like tonight.'

There was almost a full moon and they might have been phantoms as they cantered round on the dew-covered grass.

'You know I've got faith in you,' Mary reminded the horse, as she patted him. 'Mr Dewar was so tense with you all the time, wasn't he? It was like the end of the world if you ever made a mistake! Remember that time I helped you get your confidence back?'

As she took September over a few hurdles to loosen up she reflected for a while on Mr Dewar's strange obsession that Anna should win the Western Counties' Championship this year, an obsession that they had lived with for so long now and on which, in her heart, Mary pinned all the blame for the unhappiness that had come to Chestnut Farm this summer.

She certainly pinned the blame for September's accident on Mr Dewar. But was she now asking too much of the horse? This, after all, was the place where he had fallen.

When the high brushwood wall loomed up in front of them, Mary knew a moment's uncertainty: it looked so impossibly high—and beyond was the wide ditch that must also be cleared in the single jump! But September never faltered: in that first anxious moment, he was the strong one, soaring away from the turf to make a perfect clearance.

As she led him quietly back to the cottage garden and rubbed him down at the door of their big old shed, she said:

'We've nothing to fear on Monday now: except the clock. From now on we're going to practice tight turns and short run-ups. You always were fast but we've got to get you faster still.'

To make sure he did not catch a chill after his exertions she settled him in the shed that night, and the three following nights, on a bed of warm straw, and tied a blanket round him.

On Sunday afternoon, Mary waved goodbye to her father at the front gate, and set off with September for her Uncle's farm, a saddlebag packed with her overnight things and a few basics for September: brushes, hoof oil, hoof pick and a small bottle of black dye for touching up his coat if necessary.

'Goodbye, my girl. Watch out for the traffic. Have a nice time.'

Mary longed to tell her father that she was setting off on the greatest adventure of her life. Instead she just said: 'Cheerio, Dad.' Then September did an unusual thing: he turned towards Mr Wilkins, raised his upper lip and showed his teeth and gave a long, friendly whinny. It was as if to say: 'We might have some news for you when we get back, old fellow!'

They hacked along the twisting country road to Silverstock and reached Uncle Henry's farm in time for supper. That night September had a proper stable to sleep in, and Mary bedded him down early.

'No more practices, just plenty of sleep tonight. We're going to be off early in the morning.'

Uncle Henry once more borrowed the horse-box in which he had brought September to the farm seven weeks earlier, and they left after breakfast.

They reached the famous course at Imchester by midmorning. The bunting was waving, music was playing over loudspeakers, and the crowds were already streaming in.

FIFTEEN

WINNING—AND LOSING

The morning was taken up with minor events but it was the Western Counties' Championship that the spectators had come to see. If Mary had mingled with the crowds in the next four hours, she would have felt the excitement and tension building up; but, in fact, she was far too busy getting September settled in at the competitor's quarters, feeding him, grooming him and seeing that he got a little gentle exercise from time to time to loosen him up.

Uncle Henry left her to her own devices, coming back every now and then from the big refreshments marquee where he had found not only some farming friends to talk shop with but an excellent brew of Devon cider.

'All right, young 'un? No nerves?'

'Of course not, Uncle Henry,' said Mary calmly. She could not have been more unruffled by the big show atmosphere, nor even the glimpse of one or two horses and their riders who were household names in Britain. She felt so at home, here at Imchester, that she was beginning to believe that it was destiny that had brought her and September to this place. 'And September hasn't got any nerves, either—even though it's windy and he doesn't usually like the wind. Did you ever see him so relaxed?'

Henry Wilkins looked at the horse, his coat dull and matted by the black dye, and then at his niece in her faded jodhpurs, black sweater and second-hand riding hat. They made a distinct contrast to the other competitors he had seen.

'You're a girl!' he chuckled.

The one other thing that kept Mary busy before three o'clock was keeping out of Anna's way. She glimpsed her several times in the distance, walking King of Prussia round the far enclosure, and was careful not to go in that direction.

Then, an hour before the competition was due to start, she had a narrow escape. She walked over to the big tent where a buffet lunch had been provided for competitors and almost bumped into Anna and her family coming out! She dived behind two men who were standing near the entrance, deep in conversation, and bent down pretending to adjust her riding boot. For a moment she thought she must surely have been seen, but then, peering round the side of the nearest trousered leg, she could see that the Dewars were preoccupied.

Mr Dewar had paused to light his pipe and the flare from the match seemed to emphasize the steely glint in his eyes. Mary could see that Anna looked quite frightened of her father, and there was a flustered look about Mrs Dewar's face that Mary had noticed so often this summer.

'Please don't expect a miracle, Daddy,' Anna was saying. She sounded really scared. 'The wind's unsettled him, I know it has.'

'Then you'd better un-unsettle him,' said Mr Dewar. 'I've told you everything now—don't let me down, Anna.'

'Please, Richard,' said Mrs Dewar, 'don't put such a big burden—'

'Anna should know the truth, Sarah—'

Mary heard no more for the family moved on and out of earshot.

The love fostered by a lifetime of friendship with Anna had not yet died away within Mary, and now it came back to the surface. She was troubled and uneasy as she ate her lunch and found herself thinking:

I don't know what it's all about, but I feel frightened for Anna. I almost want her to win now, even if it *is* on King of Prussia. I—I've never seen her look *scared* before; she's never been scared of anything!

But it was not to be.

Anna rode out Number 7 on King of Prussia. The horse already unsettled by the wind, was even more unsettled by the aching tension in Anna's body which communicated itself to him. He refused two perfectly simple jumps, faulted several times, and was eliminated in the first round.

As Anna walked the horse out of the ring, her head bowed, Mary had an overwhelming impulse to run after her and comfort her. She fought it back. Now was not the moment to speak to Anna. She had just learnt in the most humiliating way possible that the horse she idolized was not infallible; she must be given time for the truth to sink in. Meanwhile Mary must fulfil her ambition and see to it that September acquitted himself outstandingly well in the championship.

'If we can do that,' she whispered to him, 'it could change everything. Anna will take you back to her heart, she'll see how wrong she's been all this time. She'll want *you* back for good, instead of King of Prussia, and that means we'll never be separated again.'

And in wanting September back, perhaps Anna would also want Mary back as her best friend again. That was what she was fighting for: for happiness to return to Chestnut Farm. Now it was up to her.

Mary rode out Number 23 and did a clear round.

Twelve horses went through to the second round and the jumps were raised. This time seven of the horses had faults and only five horses went through to the third round. September was one of them.

Now the jumps were being raised very high indeed and in particular a fresh layer of brushwood was added to the fence in front of the Demon's Dyke, the jump where so many horses had gone down already.

For the first time a tremor of fear ran through Mary. Having come so far she was now determined to win the championship—nothing less would do! But could they do it? Demon's Dyke was even now no higher than the replica that Mr Dewar had had built on the water meadow, but the crowds were pressing close against the barrier, only feet away from the jump, and the excitement was making them noisy. For the news had travelled fast around the course that an unknown girl on an unknown horse was among the last five.

'You mustn't let the crowd unsettle you when we get there,' she whispered, patting his neck. 'Just pretend we're back on the water meadow, jumping by moonlight—remember how you cleared it every time?'

September whinnied softly and then they were being called.

Mary hardly noticed all the other jumps, falling away easily beneath September's soaring hooves: all her concentration was for the Demon's Dyke. As she approached, the tremor returned. Why did it seem so much higher, here at Imchester, with all the spectators pressing forward, eyes popping, just waiting for disaster. . . .

Then she saw the face in the crowd: Anna's. She was staring this way, electrified, still out of breath from running all the way from the competitors' quarters where her mother had told her the news that Mary Wilkins was riding today on an unknown black horse called Good Fortune.

'Do it!' gasped Mary in the horse's ear. 'For Anna—do it!'

They were over. Three more jumps and they had a clear

round. She silently praised Anna for appearing then, and Anna's father for having had the foresight to build the dummy 'Demon's Dyke' so ruthlessly identical to how the real jump would be in these final stages of the competition.

They rested for a few minutes and then an announcement crackled over the loudspeakers and the crowds were silent.

'The winner of the Western Counties' Championship has still to be decided. Good Fortune and Stardust both had clear rounds and both returned identical times. We will now have a jump-off between these two horses. Will all spectators keep well back from the jumps, please. I repeat that. Will all spectators keep well back behind the barriers.'

The crowd was now dumb with excitement, dumb and obedient.

'First I call Number 17. Stardust, ridden by Colonel John Markham and owned by the Duke of Silverstock.'

Mary watched as Stardust, a beautiful chestnut, glided round the course. As though in a dream she saw that he had done a clear round and watched the time go up on the clock: 3 minutes 50 seconds.

Suddenly her Uncle appeared by her side, red-faced with emotion.

'You can do it, girl, you can do it,' he said in a husky voice. 'I only wish your dad were here to see it. But he'll see it on the telly tonight!'

Then the tannoy was crackling again:

'Now I call Number 23. Good Fortune, ridden by Miss Mary Wilkins and owned by Mr Wilkins.'

Mary took September round the course in an all-or-nothing burst. She knew she was risking faults, and she had a clear round to beat, but most of all she had the clock to beat. It would be useless to do a faultless round but go over the 3 minutes 50.

'Come on, boy, everything's working for us today—the crowd's with us—I can feel it—faster—faster—'

They took jump after jump, turning in the tightest figures of eight and U-turns, giving September the shortest of run-ups to each jump—but he soared over them all, even the Demon's Dyke. As they took the last jump faultlessly the crowd roared with happiness and Mary knew that the gamble had come off. The clock said 3 minutes 48 seconds.

Mary Wilkins, the unknown daughter of an unknown cowman, had won one of the most coveted show-jumping trophies in Britain—and a cheque for £3,000 for her father, as the owner of a completely obscure horse known as 'Good Fortune'.

As Mary dismounted and led September from the course, she felt weak, exhausted by her great effort, but exhilarated at the same time.

People pressed around her, shaking her by the hand; boys and girls thrust autograph books and biros under her nose. A press photographer appeared and she heard his camera click, not once, but several times. Then, all round the show ground, the loudspeakers crackled and a voice came over:

'That's it, then, ladies and gentlemen. After that very exciting jump off, this year's winner of the Western Counties' Championship is Number 23, Miss Mary Wilkins riding Good Fortune, owned by Mr John Wilkins. They completed a clear round in 3 minutes and 48 seconds. The presentation will be made on the rostrum in five minutes' time. Please allow the competitor to come to the enclosure. Thank you.'

It had all really happened! Mary flung her arms round September's neck, tears of happiness in her eyes. He nuzzled her gently.

'We've won,' she whispered. 'We've won!'

Where was Anna?

She gazed at the faces pressing in on her, but Anna's was not amongst them.

The crowd cleared a path so that she could get to the enclosure.

Foolishly, Mary half expected that she might find Anna waiting for her in the enclosure. Instead she saw only some stewards—and Colonel John Markham. He was watching, arms folded, as his groom unsaddled Stardust and started to rub him down. But he turned his head as Mary came in with September.

'Congratulations, young lady.' He was smiling. 'D'you know you've broken the Duke's six year run here, with that horse of yours? My life won't be worth living when he hears I've been beaten by a slip of a girl.'

He shook her by the hand, and she blushed. Then a deep Devonshire voice behind her told her that her Uncle Henry had arrived in the enclosure.

'I'll bet the Duke would like this fellow in his stables, Colonel Markham, sir,' he chuckled. He took Mary by the arm and she saw that his face was redder than ever and a vein was throbbing in his neck, so great was his excitement. 'I'll unsaddle him and give him a rub. You give your hair a comb, girl, you've got to be up on the rostrum in a minute. The television camera's there an' all. Didn't I say your dad would see you on telly tonight? It's goin' to be on the Regional News at six o'clock, that's what they tell me.'

When Mary walked up to the rostrum, hands reached out and patted her on the back. There was a very good turn-out indeed and a great deal of noise. This died down to a whisper when the President of the Show Jumping Association stepped forward, shook Mary by the hand, and presented her with a large silver cup and an envelope containing a cheque for £3,000 for her father.

In the silence Mary could hear the whirring of the television camera, and was dimly conscious that the President was saying kind and flattering things about her. 'A brilliant display . . . I believe we have witnessed here today . . . the birth of a new star in the world of show-jumping . . . let us all give a big hand . . .'

As people applauded, Mary's exhilaration began to be mixed with annoyance. Surely the Dewars must be here in the crowd, applauding her with the rest? In spite of everything, surely Anna would not deliberately stay away from the presentation?

But as Mary scanned the upturned faces spread below her, she suddenly felt sure that Anna was not here.

She came down from the rostrum, clutching the cup, hardly aware of the cheers and applause. She had to find Anna! She had played out the scene in her imagination so many times—now she must play it out in real life. She would not be robbed of it. She ran through it all again, for the very last time. . . .

Anna's shock when she told her that 'Good Fortune' was none other than September, the horse she had come to despise, that she believed to be dead! Anna's chagrin. She would realize that she had been quite wrong to prefer King of Prussia. She would beg her father to buy back September, and the horse would remain happily at Chestnut Farm for ever more, and Mary would never be parted from him again.

As for Mary herself—well, after what she had pulled off today, Anna would see her in a different light. She would treat her with respect, beg her forgiveness for treating her so condescendingly in recent weeks . . . in time, their friendship would be back on its old footing. Everything would be happy at Chestnut Farm again, the way it always used to be.

So it all ran in Mary's imagination. But it did not turn out like that.

She found the Dewars, alone, at the far end of the competitors' marquee. Anna was sobbing in her father's arms and he was comforting her, his face as dry and grey as the stone walls that surrounded Chestnut Farm. He looked like a man who had lost everything.

There was no new-found respect in Anna's face as she turned to Mary, only bitterness.

'If you knew your uncle owned a horse like that, don't you think it was your *place* to give us the chance of buying him and letting *me* win the championship?'

'What a nerve—' gasped Mary, but did not get any further.

'Your future's at stake, too, you know!' Anna's voice was high-pitched, almost a scream. 'You like your cottage, don't you? You once told me it was the dearest little house in the world, full of memories . . . memories of your mother . . . Well, you're going to be turned out of the cottage now, just as we'll be turned out of the farm. Your father will be out of a job—'

'Anna!' remonstrated Mr Dewar, but Mary was already at Anna's side shaking her furiously by the arm.

'What do you mean? What are you talking about?'

'My father's broke, that's what. Gone bust. The farm's going to be sold. Broken up into lots and sold. A few thousand pounds, that was all we needed—'

She started to sob. Mary had gone very pale. As Mrs Dewar put an arm round her daughter, her husband did a remarkable thing. He took Mary's hand very gently in his.

'I didn't want the news to be broken to you like this, Mary. But everything Anna says about the farm is true. You're too young to realize, but farmers have had a very bad time for the last two years, and I've had a worse time than most. I've reached the limit with the bank—they just won't lend me any more money. I know that in a few months I could have got the farm back on its feet—there's been important changes in Government policy, you see. But I haven't got a few months—'

'And—and you thought, that if Anna could win the prize—'

'Not the prize money on its own, Mary. We could have sold King of Prussia for a great deal of money if he'd won today. We—we might just have pulled through. I gambled everything on this, even sending Anna to an expensive school to be coached in riding. It was foolish of me, foolish of me—'

'But you could have helped us, Mary,' said Anna. 'I simply hate you now.'

'Don't take it out on Mary,' said Mr Dewar sharply. 'It's not like you, Anna. What's happened to you?'

'Can't you see what's happened to her?' asked Mrs Dewar in exasperation. It was the first time she had spoken. 'You've done this to her, Richard. Sent her to that *school*, turned her into a snob—the worst kind of snob because she knew in her heart that she couldn't really keep up with the other girls there. And worst of all we've put a burden on her shoulders that no young person should have been asked to carry. She—she's little more than a child, Richard. We should never have expected all this of her, never! It's made her quite, well, *different.*'

'I know,' said Mr Dewar, his voice barely audible. He let go of Mary's hand. He was overcome with despair. 'Chestnut Farm has been in our family for over 200 years. It's, well, a little piece of the English countryside that's been entrusted to me, if you like. The men who work for me, their fathers and grandfathers worked for my father and my grandfather . . .

'What I did, I did for the farm—to try and keep it intact, the way it had been passed on to me. And most of all for the men who've worked for me a lifetime, who look

116

on the farm as their home, depend on me—people like your father, Mary.'

He shook his head and covered his face with his hands.

'I've failed all of us,' he said. After a few moments he dropped his hands back to his side. 'There's really nothing more to say.'

Mary turned away, her lip trembling. How different day dreams could be from reality. She had expected this moment to be so sweet, and how bitter it was. Her father to be out of a job! Strangers—living in Primrose Cottage. Chestnut Farm to be broken up—to be sold. It was rather like being told that the world was coming to an end.

Uncle Henry came into the marquee, looking for her.

'I want you to take me home now, please, Uncle,' she said.

He became nervous as he saw the Dewars, sensed the white-faced tension all around him. He spoke without thinking.

'Right, girly. I'll get September into the horse-box.'

'September?' gasped Anna. Her eyes looked wild. 'But he's dead.'

'No,' said Mary. Her voice was sad and flat. 'My father bought him back from the slaughterhouse. He didn't want you to be offended, so he dyed his coat.'

SIXTEEN

RETURN TO HAPPINESS

Mary's father very rarely watched television. But that evening he sat on the edge of the armchair in the living-room, his gnarled hands gripping the arms tightly, and watched the Regional News on their ancient black and white television set.

He could not believe that he was watching his own daughter jumping with such brilliance on that gruelling course at Imchester; his own little Mary mounting the rostrum for the presentation, being described as a new show-jumping star in the making. Except it had to be Mary, because he would have recognized those faded old jodhpurs and battered riding hat anywhere.

He got up and turned off the set and walked across to where the trophy stood on the table. He picked it up and gazed at his daughter.

'So that's where you went today?'

Mary nodded, unable to speak. The sight of herself on television had been something of a shock.

John Wilkins then picked up the envelope containing the cheque.

'£3,000.' His fingers shook a little. 'It's yours by right.'

'No. Dad. It's made out to you. You're September's owner, you paid for him.' She turned to her Uncle Henry, who had stayed on at the cottage to watch the News. 'At least you can pay Uncle Henry back the money you owe him now!'

'What I think,' said her Uncle, 'is that you should stop looking so miserable, John, and go out and buy some champagne. If this doesn't call for a celebration, then nothing does.'

John Wilkins shook his head.

'I'd rather keep the celebrations till I've found a job,' he said.

Of course none of them knew that at that moment, less than six miles away, a portly figure was switching off the colour television set in his study, even more deeply in thought than John Wilkins.

How could they?

The next morning Curry, King and Fenton, the Silverstock estate agents and auctioneers came to survey Chestnut Farm and make a valuation, prior to putting it up for auction in six lots. They were there for most of the day, two men in tweed caps and raincoats, wearing wellingtons especially for the occasion. One of them carried a brief case from which he produced a very long metal rule on a spool from time to time, while the other one made notes.

Inside the farmhouse they measured up the rooms exactly and when they came out they used the rule to measure the exact dimensions of some of the outbuildings. For other measurements, like the length of the kitchen garden and the adjoining farm yard, they paced it out in strides.

Several of the farm workers came to watch them from time to time. Mary could not bear to watch for longer than a few minutes, especially when the man with the briefcase produced a small camera and began to take photographs of the farmhouse from many different angles.

All summer there had been undercurrents of unhappiness at Chestnut Farm and now at last it was all out in the open.

'How blind I was,' thought Mary, 'not to realize there was something like this in the wind. I was so wrapped up in myself—and September—and my stupid hurt pride over Anna—'

The shock and unhappiness was written on everyone's faces that day. Old Matthew, who was in his eighties, but still made himself generally useful around the farm, just sat outside the cowsheds, staring into space, the tears rolling down his cheeks.

As for Anna, she wandered about the farm like someone in a daze, her face white and drawn. Mary wanted to speak to her, but did not dare. Instead she went round to the back of the cottage where September was grazing and with a sponge and a bucket of hot, soapy water, she started to clean off all the black dye which had made his coat so matted and dull for the past weeks.

'At least you can look like yourself again, September,' she said.

And at least the job was a long and arduous one (the horse's coat had to be sponged down many times) and gave her something to do on this most terrible of days.

At tea-time, just as her father had sat down, the two men appeared at the back door of Primrose Cottage. They were very polite.

'We've inspected the other two cottages—we've left this one till last.'

'If we could just take a few measurements and check over its general state—it won't take us long. Then we'll be getting back to Silverstock.'

'We'd be most grateful!'

'So sorry to disturb you in the middle of tea. But you just sit right there, while we whip round.'

The words just blurred inside Mary's head. She found great difficulty in forcing her tea down as she watched the men measure up the little sitting-room and then remove the photograph of her mother while they inspected the state of the plaster on the big chimney breast.

She and her father never exchanged a word as they heard the men tramping round upstairs, their footfalls loud in the bedrooms above. It was as though strangers had already taken possession of their home and that they, eating their tea in silence, no longer had any right to be there.

But as soon as they had gone, Mary found her voice.

'The money, Dad,' she said, haltingly. 'I've been thinking about it. Couldn't you make a loan of it to Mr Dewar? Of course, I realize it wouldn't be enough on its own. But —but if we could . . .' she stumbled over the word, 'sell September, for a lot of money? I mean that was what Mr Dewar planned to do, in the beginning, wasn't it? To —to try and save the farm.'

'Aye, I've been thinking about it, too,' replied John Wilkins.

He looked very thoughtful. Mary waited with bated breath. It had taken all her courage to speak to her father like that, but his words last night had suggested that she had some claim on the money—on how it was spent.

'It would have to be such a lot of money that I doubt if anyone would pay it, Mary,' he said. 'Anything less wouldn't do—it would be throwing good money after bad. And in the meantime—' he spoke very, very slowly, '—you would have lost September.'

'But, Dad, we could at least try and advertise him and see—'

'No, Mary. We're not going to sell the horse. You're going to enter competitions with him—all over the country. The first thing I'm going to buy with that prize money is a car and trailer, to get us and the horse around to all the events you need to enter to make a name for yourself. Then I want you to get yourself some decent riding clothes and a few of the other things that other girls have—' he swallowed hard, 'which I've never been able to give you.'

So her father had decided that they were going to keep September, for good! That she was going to enter shows with him, try and make it as a show jumper! For a moment tremendous joy surged through Mary—she wanted to rush outside and tell September, hold him close to her.

Yet the joy only lasted for a moment. It was overshadowed by a feeling of melancholy. Her father did not think it was a practical proposition to try and save the farm. And he understood financial matters, far better than Mary.

'I know it's going to break your heart, girl, leaving this place,' he said, reading her thoughts. 'It doesn't make me exactly happy, either. Chestnut Farm, well it's part of me, just like it was part of your mother.' Before she had married John Wilkins, Mary's mother had worked in the dairy here, and her mother before her. 'We just haven't any choice, that's all. I'll find another job sooner or later, an' a cottage to go with it, an' that'll have to be our new home, Mary.'

He pushed his plate away and lit up his pipe, slowly and thoughtfully. Mary knew that he had more to say, Her father had never said so much to her in one go for as long as she could remember.

'I haven't made much of my life, Mary. Not as much as I would have liked—'

'Oh, Dad—' said Mary. She knew that her father had always longed for some land of his own to farm, but that Uncle Henry, being the elder of the two brothers, had been the one to inherit their uncle's small farm outside Silverstock. 'It wasn't your fault.'

'The thing that matters, Mary, is that you've got a future now. You've never had anything, not even a horse of your own. I've never even been able to pay for you to have proper riding lessons—but look at you. You've got a great future, that's what they say. Nothing's going to rob you of it. I owe you that, girl.'

Mary went over to her father and put her arms round him, and kissed him gently on the cheek. Then briskly and clatteringly she started to clear away the tea things, hoping that he would not notice the tears glistening in her eyes.

That evening when she went out to the shed to give September his oats, she pulled up short outside the door.

Anna was inside, with her arms round the horse's neck, crying softly, and whispering to him.

'I went away to school and forgot about you, didn't I, boy?' she said hoarsely. 'And from that moment on, nothing went right. I've really lost out, haven't I? I'm not going back to school, well I'm not sorry about that, but they've got to sell the farm, and they say they can't afford to keep King and—and you'll be going away, with Mary. I'll never see you again—or Mary—and—' Anna's sobs were loud now, 'and it's all no more than I deserve. Please forgive me. I know Mary won't.'

'Anna!'

Mary stepped forward into the dark shed, her face illuminated by a single shaft of moonlight. Anna turned, startled.

'Of course I forgive you!'

'Mary!' gasped Anna.

Suddenly the two girls were clinging on to each other, as though their lives depended on it.

'We'll be friends again?' begged Anna. 'We're staying in the area—Daddy's going to get a small farm, work it himself—how about you?'

'Dad would never move far from Chestnut Farm,' said Mary. She felt weak with joy. At the last possible moment, when she was least expecting it, the miracle had happened. Anna had become herself again.

'I've got to see you and September sometimes,' said

123

Anna after a while. 'It's only now—now that I've sort of lost just about everything, I realize what things are important to me and what aren't. You're important, Mary. Those girls at Kilmingdean . . . I can't even remember half their names unless I sit down and think. Please say we'll meet sometimes. You're part of everything—childhood, growing up, Chestnut Farm. So's September. You two will be the only link I'll have left with . . .' she choked a little over the words, 'with all the happy times.'

'Of course we'll meet Anna,' said Mary, wiping the back of her sleeve across her eyes. 'It's just the same for me. Exactly.'

Together in silence they fed September; he nuzzled first one girl and then the other, as though he understood exactly what was going on.

The next morning Mary glimpsed a magnificent white Range Rover bumping down the track past their cottage, heading towards the farmhouse.

She ran out to the gate.

'It must be someone interested in the farm already,' she said dolefully to old Matthew as he came by.

The old man's eyes were bright.

'That war the Duke, himself, in person,' he said. 'Now he be about the only man in Devonshire at the moment with the money.'

'With the money?'

'Aye, to buy her in one piece. Chestnut Farm won't be broke up if Duke of Silverstock buys she.'

Even as Mary was pondering the implications of the old man's words she saw Mrs Dewar coming from the farmhouse, leading a well-built portly man this way. He was a distinguished figure in a blue tweed coat and rubber boots, his hair a silvery grey colour. She realized at once that he must be the Duke of Silverstock. She also sensed from the obvious disappointment on Mrs Dewar's face that old Matthew's surmise could not be correct.

'That's Mr Wilkins' cottage,' she said wanly. 'He finished milking some time ago, I think you'll find him at home.'

Mary scuttled back up the garden path, round to the back of the house and in through the kitchen door, where her father was listening to the nine o'clock news.

'Dad!' she gasped. 'The Duke of—of Silverstock's coming. He wants to see you.'

'Aye,' said her father. He walked across and turned off the radio and then went outside to meet his visitor. Mary followed, at a safe distance.

'Good morning, Mr Wilkins. I'd like to see your horse.'

'Mary!' called her father. 'Bring September up here.'

Mary ran down to the far end of the garden where September was grazing on rough grass. She rode him bareback to the cottage, her heart pounding and her lips suddenly dry.

The Duke stared at the horse as they came up and a look of alarm crossed his face.

'No. It was the black one I was interested in. You've not sold him, have you?'

For a moment Mary felt alarmed and then she saw her father was smiling. He came across and smacked September's hind quarters as he spoke, and then gave Mary a hand down.

'This is the black one, sir. The one that beat your Stardust. We had his coat dyed black, it's a long story and ye'll not be interested in it. This is how he should look. And the name's September, by the way.'

'The colour of autumn leaves you see, sir,' said Mary shyly.

'By George!' said the Duke. He looked the animal up and down in some excitement. 'I can see it now. A magnificent animal, if I may say so.'

He turned to John Wilkins.

'I want him in my stables. I'll offer you £10,000 for him—'

'Ten—' began Mary, but was silenced by a sharp look from her father.

'I want your daughter, too, Mr Wilkins. I'm prepared to offer her a five year contract. She can work in the stables, look after the animal, ride him in competitions for me.'

'But—' began Mary, she was so excited that the whole world seemed to be spinning round, 'I haven't—'

'You haven't left school, yet. I know.' The Duke had done his homework. 'But it won't be long. Till then you can come weekends and school holidays. After that, there's a full-time job waiting for you.'

'It—it's quite an offer, sir,' said John Wilkins, finding his voice. 'A grand offer.'

'She can still live at home,' said the Duke. 'I understand you're on your own. Well, you wouldn't be losing your daughter, Mr Wilkins. The stables are easy cycling distance from here.' He frowned, as he remembered something. 'You will be staying on here? I've heard the farm's been put on the market.'

'Oh, we'll be staying here, sir,' said John Wilkins slowly. He gave Mary a look that was full of meaning. 'As a matter of fact, I don't think the farm is going to stay on the market very long.'

Nor did it. To the incredulous joy of all the Dewars, above all to Anna's, John Wilkins stepped in and saved Chestnut Farm. Accepting the Duke's offer, he had enough money to pay off all Richard Dewar's most pressing debts. This he did in return for a working partnership with Dewar. So it was that the men became co-owners of Chestnut Farm and they knew that together, with determination, they could make it prosper once again.

The friendship between Anna and Mary became even

closer than it had been before, stronger for having been through the fire, and more durable because unseen barriers had been removed. It was now a friendship between equals —in every sense of the word.

'I think it will last all our lives, don't you?' said Anna, on the day they left school. 'I've still got the shell you gave me; I'll always keep it.'

'And I your St Christopher,' said Mary solemnly. 'After all, I've got a lot of travelling to do. Haven't we both?'

For as well as being friends, the girls were beginning to attract attention—as rivals. Both were to embark on full-time careers as show-jumpers, and had already competed against each other in some important events.

Anna had been allowed to keep King of Prussia and the athletic little horse—who had had to perform under an intolerable strain that day at Imchester—soon justified her faith in him. He was improving all the time, and more than paying for his keep in prize money.

After a while, Mary even grew quite fond of the animal, who could not help his haughty expression after all, and recognized that Anna's devotion to him was as indisputable a fact of life as hers to September.

September—her very own responsibility! Mary could never quite get over the joy of it. Leaving school and childhood behind had an ecstasy all of its own, for now she could work full-time at the stables. Instead of seeing September only at the weekends and in school holidays, she saw him every day, looking after his every need, in between show jumping.

She saw less of her father these days, but she knew that he felt a deep happiness to be part owner of one of the most beautiful farms in Devon. His working day was longer than ever before, matched only by Richard Dewar's, but he looked years younger—and as fit as a fiddle on Mrs Dewar's excellent cooking.

'We're building the farm up again, slowly,' he told Mary that summer, as they stood at the edge of a field of waving corn, looking at the wooded hills beyond. 'This'll all be yours one day, yours and Anna's.' There was a bright light in his eyes. 'That's a big responsibility for two fathers, ain't it?'

Mary said nothing. She was thinking of that day when Anna had broken the news to her that she was going away to boarding school. She remembered the great fear that had gripped her, that nothing would ever be the same again on Chestnut Farm.

Well, the changes had come; but they had not been changes for the worse, not by any means.

'I think we're all happier now, Dad,' she said at last. 'Every single one of us.' Silently she added the thought: 'All thanks to a horse called September.'